Bl  I GO

MARIE REYES

© Marie Reyes. All rights reserved.

This is a work of fiction. Names, characters, businesses, places, events, locales, and incidents are either the products of the author's imagination or used in a fictitious manner. Any resemblance to actual persons, living or dead, or actual events is purely coincidental.

Chapter One

Josie looked up from her laptop as the house phone rang—rudely cutting through the peaceful silence. The shrill sound almost alien; no-one ever phoned on the land-line anymore. She glanced over at her parents, both of whom were asleep on the couch. Her mother's head lolled to the side, resting against her father's shoulder as he clutched a glass of Malbec in his hand, which threatened to spill onto his white shirt as he gently snored. Part of her wanted to wait for the caller to hang up so she could go back to her half-assed job hunting, but she didn't want her parents to wake up.

As she placed her laptop on the seat next to her, she noticed the time in the bottom right-hand corner of the screen and wondered who would call so late. It was probably a bad sign. No-one would call at this hour unless it was important. Maybe her grandmother was in the hospital again? She sighed and plodded towards the phone in the hallway, picking up the receiver, and putting it to her ear.

"Hello?" said Josie, her voice still croaky from the cold she was getting over.

"Josie, is that you?" She recognized her sister's voice, although the line was crackly, like someone was crunching aluminum foil at the other end. It was typical of her sister Tanya not to consider that her parents might be asleep. It wouldn't cross her mind to think about the time, and that people might have work to go to as she was living it up, partying in Central America.

"Having fun?" Josie asked, trying to keep the jealousy from seeping into her voice.

"I need help."

"You run out of money again or something?" Josie twirled the phone cord between her fingers whilst staring out the window onto the dark street at the front of the house. "Shall I put mom on?"

"I'm serious. You need to listen."

It was in that exact second that Josie registered the panic in her sister's voice. "What's wrong." She snapped upright from her slouched position.

"I'm in a taxi. They won't let me out. Please get dad."

Josie's heart started thumping like a jackhammer. "Dad" she called. She couldn't hear him stirring on the other side of the door. She could go and grab him, but she didn't want to leave the phone. "Dad!" she shouted louder. "Mom?"

Finally, her father opened the living room door and looked at Josie with a hazy glare. "What?" His annoyed, sleepy expression gave way to a look of concern as he locked eyes with her.

"It's Tanya. Something's wrong."

"Give me that." He grabbed the phone.

"What's going on?" He asked. There was still a hint of annoyance there, like this was some minor inconvenience in his day, and soon everything would go back to normal.

Josie couldn't hear what was being said on the other end of the line, but her father's expression told her everything she needed to know. His face dropped and his hand clutched the phone tighter. "Slow down. Now where are you?"

He went quiet, and his eyes darted around as he nodded his head. "Well, what can you see? I need street names, landmarks, anything." He grabbed the address book and pen that lived next to the phone. "Tanya. Are you still there? Hello? Tanya? Shit." He kept the phone to his ear, even though Josie could hear a dial tone blaring from the other end. Her sister was gone.

"Dad, If you don't put the phone down, she won't be able to call back." It took him a moment to register what Josie said, and he finally detached himself from the phone, slamming it back in the cradle.

"Get your laptop," he demanded.

"Why?"

"Just do it."

Josie hurried to the living room where her mom stirred on the sofa, rubbing her eyes. Confused, but not looking overly concerned. "What's up? Is it nana?"

"No. It's Tanya." Josie picked up the laptop and ran back into the hall with her mother following behind in a state of bewildered frustration, like she was being kept in the dark.

"What about her?"

Her dad was staring at the phone with his hand ready to go as if willing it to ring with the power of his mind. Although they were expecting it, all three of them jumped when the ring shrieked through the quiet house. Her father almost dropped the receiver in his hurry to pick it up.

Josie hovered as close as she could, hoping to catch a snippet of the conversation. She couldn't hear Tanya anymore. It sounded like a man's voice, but it was hard to hear over her mother babbling hysterically about calling the police. Her father silenced her with a mere look. He covered the speaker with his hand and faced them. "They want money… via wire transfer."

"I'm calling the police." Her mother announced as she dialed 911 on her cell phone.

"Not yet." He demanded. "Be quiet." He listened intently and started scrawling notes on the pad. Josie tried to see what he was writing, but his penmanship wasn't great at the best of times. He definitely had a doctor's handwriting. It looked like a child's incoherent scribblings. "How do I know you'll let her go? I want to speak to her. Put her on now." His face was bright red—his anger palpable as he shouted. It had always terrified her as a child, but wasn't sure it would be so effective on a kidnapper hundreds of miles away.

Silent tears streamed down her cheeks, pooling in the corners of her lips. The sight of her father's hands trembling only made her tears come harder and faster. Nothing rattled him. She had never even seen him cry in her entire life, but she could see he was close now. The somber wail of the dial tone spilled out of the phone. They must have hung up.

Everything had happened so fast, but now she was in slow motion, watching on helplessly as her father tried to calm down her mother. Their words faded out as a high-pitched ringing buzzed in her ears like a persistent mosquito. It was as if she had left her body and was just an onlooker, disassociated from what was happening. Despite her father's protesting, her mother called the police, and he had to take over the call as her mother could barely speak. Her chest heaved, and it looked as if her heart may explode as every bit of color drained from her face.

He gave the cops the limited detail that he had: roughly where she was, that she had got into a taxi, and that the taxi driver drove her somewhere secluded and demanded that a vast sum of money be sent to a Mexican bank account via a wire transfer. It couldn't be real. This couldn't be happening. Josie took a deep breath and tried to talk herself out of the blind panic that consumed her.

She opened her laptop and muttered obscenities when it took forever to load. The blank page and turning blue circle taunted her from the screen. *"Come on."* Surely the World Wide Web could help her. The Internet had all the answers, didn't it?

The only Internet searches she could find, all related to scams. Not this situation. None of the testimonies referred to people who had actually spoken with their loved one before the kidnappers demanded money. This was real. This was happening.

Her father raised his voice. "But they said they would kill her if I went to the police, if I didn't pay. I can't just sit here and do nothing like some schmuck." He yelled down the phone.

Josie trawled through her sister's social media accounts, hoping for some hint that this was all some joke, but all she came across was the typical vacation snaps: cocktails by the pool, groups of travelers snapped in midair, their limbs splayed out in some ridiculous position as they jumped, white sand beaches, waterfalls. She scrolled down to see earlier pictures. Her sister petted a Llama with vast sandy mountains stretching out in the desert landscape in the background. There was nothing that would help—nothing in the last few hours.

Chapter Two

The road seemed to go on forever, and even though he was walking downhill, he was still panting like a dog in a hot car. No doubt he was berry-red by now and glistening with sweat as his clammy hands swiped along his phone screen to zoom into his destination. It wasn't far now; mere meters away. Another car drove past, blasting him with the heat from the exhaust. Apart from a steady stream of cars, there was little else going on, and no one else walked down the street he was on. He had stumbled upon the quietest part of Tijuana, which he was grateful for. A terracotta-colored house came into view from the adjoining street. Finally, according to the map on his phone, it was just coming up on the right.

Veterinaria—the big-bold letters appeared in blue on the banner above the shop.

Michael stopped and wiped sweat off of his forehead with the back of his hand. A combination of the unrelenting heat and nerves had sent his sweat glands into overdrive. He had never been more anxious in his life, and that was saying something. The building formed part of a mini strip mall. It was peaceful, and he could see the mountains in the distance from his elevated position. He couldn't help but laugh when he noticed that positioned above the veterinarian surgery, up a tall flight of metal stairs, was a psychiatrist's office. It was a little late for that now.

Sunlight bounced off of the white buildings, so he put his sunglasses back on after wiping sweat and sun-lotion off the lenses with the fabric of his t-shirt, and leaned against a metal post while he practiced what he was going to say. He pulled away the t-shirt that clung to his back to get some airflow to his skin as he psyched himself up to go inside. As he crossed the small parking lot, the shade of palm trees momentarily provided him with shelter from the persistent sun, and he took a deep breath. Stood in front of the glass door, he willed himself to go inside. There was no point dragging this out. In and out. Get it over with.

He was met with two rows of shelves as he entered, and the woman at the end of the store stood behind the till, giving him a nod of acknowledgment. He was glad she didn't speak to him, and he wondered if he was even capable of getting words out at that moment. In his pocket was a picture of what he was looking for. The drug he wanted went under a handful of different brand names and he managed to find photographs of the various colored packaging online in case he struggled to find it as all the labels were in Spanish, for products he had never had a use for: dog worming tablets, flea treatment, antibiotics and such. His eyes scanned the shelves, briefly hovering over each box. It didn't seem to be on this side of the shop, so he moved over to the next aisle. The scent of disinfectant and other cleaning products stung his nostrils as he browsed, and he started to feel queasy.

What if he couldn't find it? He didn't know if he could bring himself to ask. He could always visit another vet. The print-out had started to fall apart in the creases where his sweat had soaked into the paper. As he turned to the next shelf, a red and white box stood out to him. It even had Pento on the label. This was it. A huge surge of relief rose within him, and despite the morbid nature of his purchase, he felt elated and had to resist the urge to do a little happy dance in the middle of the store. Somehow — he thought the hard part was over. He couldn't get over the fact that this drug people call, death in a bottle, wasn't even behind the counter, and that anyone could walk in and buy it. Even though it was perfectly legal in Mexico, his throat was as dry as the desert as he walked towards the counter with his box.

Hopefully, there wouldn't be any questions. As casually as he could muster, he put the box down in front of the woman and reached for his wallet. He tried to look directly at her, like she had nothing to be suspicious of, but her eyes lingered on him for longer than he would have liked. He couldn't maintain eye-contact any longer, and she took his tattered note and ran it through the cash register. He snatched up the change that she placed on the counter and a coin slipped through his fingers. The sound of the edge of the coin striking the floor seemed deafening in the quiet store, and Michael cringed as the sound of it rolling across the ground seemed to go on forever.

"Los siento. Gracias." He grabbed the box of Pentobarbital and rushed to the door, leaving the runaway coin on the floor. Once outside, he didn't stop. He power-walked across the road until he was a safe distance away, propped himself up against a wall and took a deep breath.

"You did it," he said to himself as he unzipped his backpack and stashed the package right at the bottom. Now he could relax.

Chapter Three

The hostel was a breath of fresh air and Michael was glad to be done with Tijuana and Mexico City. His plan was to work his way overland, finishing up in Cancún, and he was now in the charming city of Puebla. He sat on one of the unstable wicker chairs which made up the hostel's collection of eclectic furniture and placed his cold beer on the wooden table in front of him, coated in the remnants of people's sticky drinks. Music from one of the other guest's phones drifted across the rooftop terrace as he looked out over the city, his eyes draw to the towering spires of the cathedral. He lifted his drink, almost bringing the table up with it, and wondered what the hell had been spilled on it, glue?

A chill ran through him as a breeze brushed passed. It was the first time since he arrived in Mexico that he hadn't been hot, and it took him a moment to remember why. The altitude made Puebla a much cooler place. There was something about gazing over the colonial architecture as the light changed that made him feel at ease for the first time since he had got there. Colorful Talavera tiles ran along the side of the bar, mesmerizing him with their patterns.

"Do you mind if I sit?" A girl asked. Her two friends stood behind her. She had an accent he couldn't place, definitely European though.

"Go for it." He nudged the chair out for her with his foot as her friends gathered two more spare chairs from other tables. She sat down, placed her pack of cigarettes on the table and tucked her mousy blonde hair behind her ear.

"Where are you from?" she asked.

Ah yes, the standard traveler questions. Where are you from? Where have you been? Where are you going next? It beat people asking what you did for a living, a question he never liked giving the answer to. There was no way to make data entry sound exciting.

"I was born in California, but I've lived in lots of different states in my time."

"Oh cool," she said. He couldn't tell if she was feigning interest, but she seemed genuine enough.

"And you?." He watched her light up her cigarette.

"I am Anna, from Denmark."

"I'm Michael, nice to meet you." He took a sip of his beer so he would have something to do with his hands.

As her friends sat down, they introduced themselves. Freja and Aleksander. He tried to commit their names to memory. With a glint in his eyes, Aleksander pulled out a tattered pack of cards from his pocket. "Anyone fancy a drinking game?" A broad smile spread across his face. Michael wasn't sure what it was, but he instantly liked this guy. "I have a little something." He pulled out a bottle of some piss-colored liquid from the rucksack that rested at his feet.

"I'm in." Michael could do with a little social lubricant. He watched as Aleksander arranged the cards in a circle, with a gap in the middle in which he positioned a tall glass. "I know this one. Kings?"

"Kings, ring of fire. It has many names. You pick the first card."

"Why thank you." He teased a card out from the ring. "King." He held the card out for everyone to see and made a discard pile. He dribbled some beer into the glass in the center of the table for some unlucky person to drink later.

Anna slipped a card out and looked blankly. "I don't know what this one is?" Her delicate features scrunched up in confusion.

"Nine is rhyme." Aleksander said.

"Ah, okay. So I just say any word?"

"Anna, we played the other day. Do you not remember?"

"Too many rules. Okay, okay. Um."

"Just pick a word." Freja laughed. "Okay, I think we need a drink while you think rule. You're taking so long."

"Okay. Beer. Beer is the word."

They went around the group: deer, steer, career, tear, queer, shear. Michael was stumped after that and gladly accepted defeat with a burning shot of tequila washed down with a swig of beer. Freja was next and drew a five. Thumb master. Next Aleksander drew a four. "Whores!" He shouted, and everyone on the rooftop glared at them.

"Alex, shut up." Freja shoved him, almost knocking him off his chair.

He pointed at her, "You drink, girls drink. It's the rules."

As Freja drank she subtly placed her thumb on the table, and Michael and Anna quickly followed suit. "Now you drink!" She ordered. "Karma."

***

The city took on a beautiful glow in the fading light as the colors of the vibrant buildings intensified. Each table had a ceramic candle holder, and Aleksander lit the candle inside. "Romantic." He winked at Michael.

"So forward. We've only just met." Michael joked as he picked up another card. "Jack. What is Jack again?"

"Make up a rule."

"No cursing." Michael chose this rule as he knew he was useless at sticking to it.

"We are going to Cholula in the morning if you want to come. It's early, though. You can book at front desk." Aleksander offered.

"For sure. Thanks for the invite." Michael had that feeling he would always get after a few drinks. It started with a warm feeling in his chest, which spread throughout his body into a tingling sensation that travelled down his limbs as the tension melted out of him. Colors looked that bit more vibrant and the surrounding air seemed alive with possibility. A goofy grin spread across his face, and he didn't care.

The rest of the game was a blur until Michael drew the last king. The waterfall card. He looked at the large glass in the center covered in smudged fingerprints, filled with warm beer, tequila, and wine. He tentatively picked it up and screwed up his face as he brought the glass to his lips, trying to ignore the sickly smell of the liquid inside.

***

The first thing that hit him was the pain. An unholy trinity of shooting, throbbing and stabbing pain attacked his head from all angles. Heat radiated from his forehead as if it were on fire. Bright light felt like it was searing through his eyelids and despite his best efforts, he could not will himself back to sleep. It hurt to swallow as his throat was so dry and he sunk his head into the pillow. It was so hot, yet he was covered in a blanket. Fragments of his dream came back to him. He had been lost in the desert, dying of thirst, and an oasis appeared in the distance—lush green plants, and rippling water. As he hurried towards it, his feet sank into the sand. It seemed to get further and further away as he waded through the burning sand. It didn't take a genius to work out why he'd had that dream.

As he shifted in the bed, he felt the solid heat of another body next to his. He forced his eyes open a crack to see he was in a dorm room, not his own private room. It was only then that he also realized he had no clothes on. He could see his T-shirt strewn over one of the steps of the bunk bed ladder and groaned as he leaned to pick it up. The body next to him stirred.

"Hi," A squeaky, timid voice. A face he did not recognize.

"Morning." He replied, trying to play it cool. "So… last night."

"It was fun. Everyone loved your song." She giggled.

"My song?" He asked. Hoping the fog would lift, and he could recollect anything after drinking the glass of assorted alcohol. He had that sinking feeling that he had done something awful, or humiliating, but had no idea what it was.

"Michael. There you are." Aleksander appeared in the doorway. His voice was annoyingly chirpy. "I've been looking all over for you. You're going to miss the bus." He moved around with the energy of a toddler after a sugar binge, and Michael was the exhausted parent begging for just 10 more minutes sleep.

Even though he felt like he was seconds from death, Michael would rather get some fresh air then deal with awkward goodbyes with the stranger he had woken up with. "Shit," he mumbled to himself as he felt around the bed for his boxer shorts.

Aleksander was milling outside the dorm room on the upstairs landing with the others, when Michael emerged.

"We thought you'd abandoned us," said Freja. "How are you feeling this morning?" Freja wore a bohemian flowery dress, flip-flops and various bangles, and hair neatly braided to the side. All of them looked dewy and fresh faced.

"I think you know the answer to that," he croaked.

"Here. I have another one in my bag." Anna passed him a bottle of water. It must have been poured straight from the water cooler because it had beads of condensation dripping down the side.

"You are literally an angel. I don't know how to thank you." Michael grabbed the bottle, unscrewed the lid and downed half of the water in a second. It was possibly the best drink he had ever had in his entire life.

"We seriously need to go now." Freja headed down the stairs, her flip-flops slapping against the hard floor and echoing in the stairwell. When they got to the bottom of the stairs, several people were congregated in the reception area, and Michael tiptoed around the obstacle course of backpacks that littered the floor, trying not to move to suddenly. Even the slightest movement made it feel like his brain was rattling around in his skull.

"Nice of you to join us." The tour guide greeted them. "Okay guys. Time to go." He ushered the group outside.

Chapter Four

After three days in Puebla, Michael moved on to the equally beautiful city of Oaxaca. By that time, he had met many Aleksanders, Annas, and Frejas. In the few days he had spent in Mexico so far, many people had come and gone. It didn't take long for them to become interchangeable, for their faces to all blend into one. The first goodbye was emotional, and each subsequent goodbye was less heartfelt, and more a formality. He spent his days in Oaxaca eating and drinking, sometimes with company, sometimes solo. At home, he would never have entertained the idea of eating alone. It was unheard of. He didn't know of anyone else that did either. Considering how much he enjoyed people watching, it didn't sit right with him that he would let strangers' opinions of him stop him from doing something he wanted to do. Was he that weak?

He watched them pass by, completely absorbed in their lives as if no one else existed except them and the other people in their little bubbles. They were the main characters of their own stories, yet had no idea how inconsequential their stories were in the grand scheme of things.

***

He collapsed in his bed after a long day of aimless walking along the streets—no longer delighted by the colorful buildings, vibrant energy and ruins. Everything got old in the end. He lay on his back and stared up at a brown water stain on the ceiling as he tried to get comfortable. He wondered if the mark on the ceiling was from a leak, and whether he could expect to have water drip down on him in his sleep. As he looked up at the stain, he could start to make out shapes in it, like when he used to find shapes in the clouds as a kid as he laid on the grass. Where the water crept across the ceiling in fingers, it looked like two rabbit ears, and once he saw that, he could make out the feet. Why did humans have to try to find meaning in every little thing? Meaning where there isn't any. It was probably something to do with survival. Some innate thing you are born with. It was the reason people would find the image of the Virgin Mary burned onto slices of toast. We couldn't cope with the notion that everything was just chaos. He shifted on the thin mattress and faced the bare wall. He needed to rest up for his trip to the Hierve-el-Agua in the morning.

After sleeping for most of the journey, the shared taxi lurched on the bumpy mountain road, jolting Michael awake as his head banged against the window.

"Good afternoon sleepy head." A British voice greeted him. He wanted to say her name was Amanda but couldn't quite remember. The last couple of days had been a blur.

"Where are we?" he asked. He would catch a glimpse of mountains in the distance, only for the van to weave the other way, blocking other side. The satisfying crunch of loose rocks under his boots accompanied him all the way up the hill. As they reached the crest of the peak, Michael looked down to see shimmering pools below. Natural springs encased in ripples of white, salty rock. The shallower pools looked white where you could see the salt below the water, with one large central pool that was a brilliant pale blue. Light reflected off the perfectly still mirror of water and the glass-like surface seemed to just drop off the edge like an infinity pool, as if he was stood at the end of the world. Above the water, the panorama of dark green, tree-covered mountains in the distance rose and fell like waves. The thing that caught his eye was a lone tree sticking out from behind the turquoise pool, protruding from the rock as if it had broken through. The dark brown—almost black branches stuck up into the air like parched claws reaching for the sky. He drank it in, trying to capture the moment in his head so he could hold on to it for as long as he had left. It didn't take long for before the pool was overrun with by people taking selfies. They strategically positioned themselves and gazed into the horizon while getting someone to take that perfect 'candid' shot. Michael watched people in the water. Dancing and posing. He just lay on the rock like a cold-blooding reptile sunning themselves. the view.

"We're almost there."

The van struggled up the incline, rocking from side to side as its tires traversed the rough ground below, and Michael looked out as the mini-bus kicked up clouds of dust that drifted in through the crack in the window. The hollow feeling of hunger gripped his stomach, and he leaned forward as a wave of nausea peaked. The terrain started to level out, and they reached the parking lot. It was a relief to finally be still, and Michael hurried to get off of the bus. He squeezed past the other passengers as they took their time gathering their things. He needed to be out in the non-recycled air.

It was only a short uphill walk from the van. The early afternoon sun caressed one side of his face and a breeze, the

The heat radiating from the stone warmed him from below, and the sun toasted him from above.

None of it looked real. It was as if he existed in a postcard, yet at the same time, everything felt heightened. He was finally present in the moment.

Life often tried to trick him like this. Every now and then it would show him something beautiful. It would try to convince him that there was a point to all suffering—a reason that could make working a job you hate, for most of your waking hours, worthwhile. It was a liar, a very good one—well, it fooled most of the population. The moments like this, the moments where life seemed worth living, they were the minority. The majority was work, housework, more work, commuting, coming home to watch the latest tragedy on the news, consuming. Repetition, repetition, repetition all culminating in an inevitable, and probably painful death.

The British girl tapped him on the shoulder. "Michael, are you not going in?"

"Yeah. Soon." He couldn't tear his eyes away from the mountains. There was something about mountains. Even though they were just enormous pieces of rock, they somehow signified adventure. They made him feel small, but in a good way for once.

"We are booking a cabana for the night. They are quite cheap, and apparently a great way to avoid the crowds. Imagine this at sunset." She stretched her arm out like a weather girl, presenting him with the stunning panorama as if she thought he was too blind to notice it before now.

"Yeah. Thanks. I'd like that." He gave her a smile, that for once, he didn't have to force.

***

Now their accommodation was booked for the evening, Michael could relax. He took off his boots that he had brought in one of Puebla's many shoe stores to replace his battered canvas sneakers. The new-unbroken material had taken its toll on his ankles and as he took off his socks, he let the open air sooth his feet. The cool water of the spring did the rest, and he let out an unadulterated moan as the refreshing ripples danced around his legs.

"This is the life right?" The Australian from his mini-van said, as he sat down beside him.

"Hell yeah." Michael didn't have to fake enthusiasm. "Sorry I didn't catch your name."

"Jerry." The burly, bearded Aussie opened up a paper bag and directed the contents at Michael. "Chapulines?"

"Come again?" Michael foolishly hadn't learned a lick of Spanish and had to get by only on what he had gleaned from television shows.

"Grasshoppers."

"Nah I'm okay. You knock yourself out though."

"Ah come on mate. Live a little." He dragged his small backpack from behind him. "We can wash em down with this." He unzipped his pack and pulled out a thin bottle of mezcal.

"Okay, fine, you convinced me." He leaned forward to closer inspect the contents of the bag. Brown, unappetizing, their stick like limbs still sticking out, Michael plucked one up and shoved it straight in his mouth whole. If he was doing this, he wanted it over and done with. The texture alone made him gag. He held his nose so he could avoid the taste.

"No, that's cheating," said Jerry right before popping one in his mouth with a casualness as if he was eating a potato chip. He exaggerated the crunches and opened his mouth to show Michael the half chewed gooeyness inside.

"Oh god, stop." Michael retched.

"Here you go mate." Jerry took pity on him and passed him the mezcal.

After a good quarter of the bottle, Michael walked across the pool and climbed up the other side. Although it looked like the water just dropped off the edge, there was more beyond the pool. Massive platforms of pale bulbous rock jutted out overlooking the mountain vista and seemed to flow down the side of the mountain, like the water that had formed them. Michael assumed it was created by a long, slow buildup of mineral deposits left by the waterfall that had once been there, but he couldn't be bothered to ask a guide.

By the time most of the day tourists had left, they had the sunset to themselves. As the sun disappeared behind the mountains, dusky orange tinged with purple reflected in the perfectly still pools to the point where you couldn't differentiate the water from the sky. All he could liken it to was one of those screen-saver pictures that had been adjusted until it no longer looked real, but instead, a fantastical, idealized version of what it really was. No filter could create what he was seeing now. Day-drinking in the heat had given him a mild headache, but he didn't care.

There was something inexplicably magical about a sunset, until his brain felt the need to remind him that the sunset he was seeing was just where the light had further to travel in the evening, and the blue light waves couldn't make it through the atmosphere, leaving the longer, red wavelengths visible, at least, that was how he understood it. Nothing magical about it.

Chapter Five

After a whirlwind few days in Chiapas and Campeche, Michael arrived in Tulum. It was nice to look at, but lacked the authentic charm of other places he had visited. It was dark by the time his taxi pulled up at the hotel. He had booked the plushest hotel he could find for his budget, and the only thing he was looking forward to in that moment, was his head hitting the pillow. He was so tired he didn't even check what denomination the note was that he gave the driver as a tip. The driver looked surprised and said nothing, so he assumed it was a lot. He grimaced as his bag straps rubbed against his sun-burnt shoulders and he lumbered up the marble steps, his legs stiff, yet rubbery as jelly at the same time. It was jarring to go from the darkness to the bright hotel reception. The lobby was all dazzling shiny surfaces, from the polished floor, to the mirrored walls. Without saying a word, he put the piece of paper he had printed with his reservation details on the front desk and the young male receptionist picked it up and started inputting details into their computer system, their head bobbing with the rhythmic clacking of keys.

"Fourth floor. If you need anything, let me know. Enjoy your stay at Casa Sands." He kept his spiel brief, probably picking up on Michael's exhaustion. He slid the key card across the desk. It was tucked in a paper sleeve with the Wi-Fi password printed on it.

"Thanks." Michael slipped the card in his shorts pocket and shuffled towards the elevator as a gaggle of high-pitched girls ran in front of him. He pushed the button for the fourth floor and tapped his foot as he waited for the elevator to come down. The light seemed to hover on the third floor for ages. *Come on.* He was like a race-horse champing at the bit, when the door pinged for the ground floor. A large group of twenty-some-things flooded out of the elevator when it opened, no doubt on their way out for a night of heavy drinking. Their energy was tiring just to watch. After the last person emerged, Michael slipped in and leaned against the metal railing at the back. The mirrored surfaces made the small space feel less claustrophobic, and he caught a glimpse of himself. His hair was all over the place, shoulders slumped and dark circles under his eyes. He had looked better. Why wasn't the elevator moving? It would help if he pressed the button. He reached over to the panel and the doors started opening again.

A girl in a coral blouse rushed into the elevator, breathing heavily, and pressed the third floor button. She glanced over at him and granted him a small smile, barely perceptible—such a serious face for someone at a party-resort—as if she was here on a business trip. Her poker straight long brown hair shined in the harsh artificial lighting. Michael straightened up. There was always something awkwardly intimate about being in such an enclosed space with a stranger. He considered small talk to break the silence, but decided against it as the muffled sound of the hydraulics whirred in the background.

She looked so deep in thought, that he couldn't glean anything by looking at her—a closed book. He looked down, not wanting her to think he was checking her out or anything like that. Suddenly he started humming. It wasn't a conscious action—it just came out. Obviously his brain had tried to remedy the awkward silence—by doing something even more awkward. Not sure what he was humming, he started improvising. Maybe sewing together melodies from random songs he had heard in the taxi. His voice sounded far too loud in the small space and he started trailing off.

Once she got out on her floor Michael breathed a sigh of relief as he was alone again, and he resumed his slouch until the fourth floor. 418.

His floor didn't seem to resemble the rest of the hotel. It smelled faintly like stale alcohol and cigarettes as he walked towards his room, and he could hear other rowdy guests from behind their doors.

He looked at the door numbers as he walked along the corridor. His room was at the end and through a heavy set of doors. He slotted the key card in the mechanism and waited for the light to turn green. It was pitch black until he turned the main light on. He followed his hotel routine of putting his bag on the bed and opening the curtains to check out the view, to find out he had got lucky this time. His room overlooked the main swimming pool framed by palm trees, and the surrounding lights made the water glow a fluorescent turquoise. White plastic chairs were laid out in rows on each side of the pool, and he watched as a boy plucked a girl from her chair, throwing her over his shoulder and swinging her into the pool. Her screams of protest went ignored, and she flailed around in the water as her friends laughed, before jumping into the pool to join her. He felt odd spying on them so closed the curtains and inspected the room. So, this would be the place where he would take his last breath, and he couldn't think of anywhere better. There was nothing left to worry about. The future was a burden he didn't have to pull him down. All that was left, was the here and now. He walked back to his bag and unzipped it, pulling out clothes and toiletries until he got to the bag buried in the bottom. The box inside looked so innocent, like it could be cough syrup, or something equally innocuous. It didn't look like something that could kill a man in minutes. He opened the lid and pulled out the bottle, examining the contents. Just a clear liquid—nothing to see here. Also in his bag, next to the Pentobarbital, was some mescaline he had acquired from a man in Chiapas. He offered the mescaline in its pill form, which would have been a lot easier to take, but Michael wanted to prepare his gag reflex, so that by the time he had to take his Pentobarbital, he would be used to swallowing bitter things. Although he was so tired he was tempted to take some mescaline there and then. It's not like he had anything else to do. The room looked clinical and sparse, with none of the personality of the hostels he had stayed in before. He took advantage of the closet and started hanging up his clothes. This was his final destination; might as well make it his own. He laid out his toiletries in the bathroom. Shower gel, razor, tooth paste, tooth brush. In the hostels he had to lug his stuff back and forth between his room and the shared bathrooms.

He made the mistake of leaving his stuff in there before and the next time he came to brush his teeth and shower some skint backpacker must have stolen it.

The whirring air-con made a calming background noise. He couldn't stand true silence, as it let his thoughts have free-reign. As he turned on the shower, the sound of the high-powered streams of water hitting the porcelain below relaxed him even further. After putting some music on his phone and placing it on the sink, he hopped into the flow of cool water—the perfect temperature to sooth his angry red shoulders. Cascades of water ran down his torso, washing away the grime of the last two days. Somewhat energized from the cleansing shower, Michael donned a complementary bathrobe. This was the life. He grabbed a menu from the writing desk and browsed through the pages. Today was a room service day. Despite the exotic options available, he opted for a beef burger with mulato-chilli cheese.

***

Clean, and with a full stomach, Michael felt renewed. He continued to play music, got the baggie of mescaline and walked over to the kettle. As he waited for it to boil, he held up the packet to his face and looked at its dry, brown contents, trying to remember how much the guy had said to take. He aired on the side of caution and put a little into his cup before topping it up with the freshly boiled water. He swirled the mixture, watching it turn a yellowy brown—h*ere goes nothing.*

He sat on the soft bed waiting for the drug to kick in, and not sure what to expect. He had dabbled in hallucinogenics before, in his younger days, and hadn't had a bad reaction yet. Instead of just waiting, Michael walked up to the closet and went through his limited selection of clothes. This was a fancy place, but all the other guests seemed to be casual, so he opted for his usual shorts and T-shirt—the last fresh pair he had. He went back to the bed and laid back against the plump pillows to rest his eyes for a moment.

When Michael opened his eyes, he knew time had passed, how much, he wasn't sure, but the room looked different somehow. After taking a couple of minutes to remind himself where he was and to make sense of his surroundings, he felt the need to get out of the room. As he collected his things and walked out the door into the hallway, a tingly buzz traveled up and down his arms as if the air around them felt alive, and he could sense each individual particle vibrating. The world in front of his eyes felt crisp and more vivid than usual. He wanted to touch everything. As he approached the elevator he became aware that he had a strange smirk on his face, but couldn't help it. The more he tried to keep a straight face, the more he smiled, and it took all his willpower to stop himself from bursting out laughing. There was no one in the elevator when it arrived at his floor, and as the elevator dropped down below him, his stomach lurched. The face looking back at him from the mirrored walls did not look like his own, and the longer he looked at it, the more distorted it became. It was him, but with small differences, just similar enough that it was still recognizable as him, but just different enough that something was clearly not right. It was the eyes. When he decided he couldn't look at them anymore, the ping of the elevator reaching the ground floor made him jump.

Avoiding eye contact with the other guests waiting to get in the elevator, he slipped by them, past the reception desk and straight out the doors into the warm night air. The sound of insects chirping and distant conversations droned in the background. Bushes and red tropical plants lined the building, and he followed the path towards the sound of voices. When he got to the end of the wall, he turned to the right and the swimming pool revealed itself to him. The pool area was full of young people talking way louder than they needed to. Michael missed his twenties. Everything seemed just that little more rosy then. In his twenties he still had the hope that he could make something of his life, that anything he did mattered.

The hotel bar overlooked the pool. Despite the luxuriousness of the hotel, the bar had a rustic vibe. A straw roof, wooden chairs and tables, and cocktails flowing with free abandon. He couldn't help but smile when he remembered he had paid for all drinks to be included. There was only one free table left, so he planted himself down and started looking through the drinks menu. Determined to get his money's worth, Michael ordered two cocktails, and whilst he waited for them to be made, the buzzing of the blender started up.

He looked over at the drinks on the table next to him. The selection of drinks seemed to cover all the colors of the rainbow. A mojito stuffed with green mint, a pale-yellow pina colada crowned with a bright slice of pineapple, a strawberry daiquiri bejeweled with dark red fruits and the orange and red ombre of a tequila sun-rise.

The bartender came back with his drinks. A wide salt-rimmed glass of tried-and-true margarita, and something mysterious topped with half a purple passion-fruit. Now he sat still, the slight movement of his surroundings became more apparent. Nothing seemed stable, and he felt as if his hands were sinking into the table.

"Do you mind if I sit on the end of your table? There's nowhere else to sit."

He hadn't even noticed her approach and tried to find his words. "Oh, yeah. Sure. Yes." He blabbered. The lady put her laptop on the table and he recognized her peachy-colored blouse and sleek hair from earlier. "You were in the elevator." He was unsure why he said that and was certain she would be creeped out by him remembering her.

"Oh yeah. Hi. I'm Josie."

"Nice to meet you. You here on business?" he asked, glancing at the laptop.

"Not exactly." She didn't elaborate and ordered a beer from the bartender in perfect Spanish, well he assumed. It sounded perfect.

She pointed at his drinks. "They look nice."

"Yeah, I thought, when in Rome. Although it feels a bit weird having girl cocktails while you're having a beer."

"I don't subscribe to gendering drinks." Her face lit up with a smile.

"Well I do. I take it very seriously."

"Okay then, what gender is a bourbon?"

"Male of course, next."

"What about a mojito? I know it's a cocktail but—"

"It's a tomboy. Next."

"Cider?"

"Oh, you're throwing a curve ball in there. Male. Next."

"But, it's so sweet." She looked bemused, but like she was enjoying herself.

"Still male. Next."

"Wine."

"Female, obviously. Come on, I'm no rookie, give me a tricky one."

The bartender arrived with her beer and placed it on the table with a napkin underneath, which soaked up the remnants of previous drinks that had been spilled on the table. Reflections from the pool danced across Josie's face and he had to stop himself from staring as strange shapes shifted across her, making her ripple.

"I was thinking of ordering the chilaquiles." Her mouth distorted in an unnatural way as she spoke, and Michael's brain tried to make sense of what was happening. "Are you okay?" Her voice anchored him and her face went back to normal.

"Listen. I don't want to freak you out or anything, but I took some mescaline earlier, so I might act a bit weird."

"Ah man." She laughed. "You're in for an interesting night."

"You've tried it? He asked, hoping for some wise guide to talk him through it."

"Hell no. I've read about it though." She leaned in closer to him, studying his face like he was a science experiment. "Are you hallucinating right now?"

"No exactly. Kinda."

"What can you see now?" Her chair scraped across the concrete as she pulled in closer.

"Nothing looks right. It's hard to describe. You kind of look like a cartoon character right now."

"A cartoon character." She looked amused. "Like Jessica Rabbit, or Elmer Fudd? What are we talking about here?"

"Definitely the Jessica Rabbit end of the spectrum. And your eyes are a bit swirly. I don't know. It's hard to describe."

"I take it you're not up for food then?"

"I ate back in the room." His mouth dried up as if he had run out of words for the day. "I think I have to go." As everything seemed to spin, his room seemed a million miles away.

"You don't look so good. Do you want me to help you to your room?"

"You don't have to." He protested, slightly embarrassed, his stomach tossing and turning like a dingy in a squall.

"Well, I'm not giving you the choice. I'm not leaving you in this state." She stood up and offered for him to lean on her as he got up.

"Why are you being so nice to me?" He heard his own voice, and it sounded pathetic.

She tilted her head to one side as if deep in thought. "People need to look out for each other. It's not safe."

It's not safe. The words sent a chill down his spine and felt like a warning.

"Come on you. You're gonna be fine." Her voice was reassuring. She sounded so certain in her words. Maybe he would be fine. She guided him feebly up the path like a nurse taking an elderly person to the bathroom.

"Now this is a tricky bit," she said as they navigated the steps that felt twice as tall as earlier. The lobby was painfully bright, and Michael looked down at his feet until he was safely in the elevator. "Are you going to be alright if I leave you here?" she asked when she reached her floor.

"Yes. Thank you. I'm sorry."

She got out and turned back to him. "Don't be sorry." She gave him a wave before the doors slid shut behind her.

The corridor seemed to get longer and longer as Michael walked towards his room, like something from a Hitchcock movie. He hurried his pace as his stomach protested, burst through the door, bolted to the bathroom and emptied the contents of his stomach.

Chapter Six

The grounds of the hotel resort looked less glamorous in the cold light of day, without the romantic glow of fairy lights. As he passed the pool, he screwed his face up at the bodies of floating insects that had met their demise there. Having only managed about an hour or two of sleep, he was certain he looked like shit, but he couldn't wait. He had to thank Josie for looking after him. His head was a little sore, but he had been expecting much work. Sunglasses shielded his delicate eyes from the intense morning light, and everything was a murky shade of brown through the lenses.

Hordes of people swarmed around the pool, staking their claim by laying their beach towels across chairs and then heading to the bar to stock up on drinks. Despite the early hour, plenty of people already had a cocktail or two in their hands. One man looked like he had already raided the bar and leaned over, slurring at an uncomfortable-looking woman whose eyes darted around desperately for a distraction.

He would never find her at this rate. The bar was full of people vying to get served before everybody else. It was a free for all with no order to be seen. None of them were her. It might have been quicker to grab a coffee in his room, but he was already downstairs now, so he may as well enter the fray.

By the time Michael managed to get served, most of the people other customers had already left for the pool, the beach, or one of the many excursions the hotel arranged. He ordered himself a coffee, and the earthy smell of those freshly ground beans woke him up a little. He sat at the back of the bar watching each new person as they came in and took a sip of his steaming coffee, enjoying the peace. Today, he only had one goal, and in the meantime, he could revel in the pleasure of doing nothing in particular. He'd spent the last few days hiking, swimming in the underground caves of cenotes, and clambering on ruins, and now, was time to relax. The palm fronds swayed in the distance as his eyes followed them backwards and forwards as he zoned out.

A stab of anxiety jabbed him out of nowhere. The peace and relaxation that made him let his guard down, and his body brought him back down to earth—reality waits for no man.

He pictured his last few moments, hoping he would feel relief, but with a strong inkling that survival mode might kick in to fuck everything up. He knew if he listened to that doubting voice inside him, that he would regret it. He couldn't go back to his normal life. There was nothing for him there. If he put the do not disturb sign up, hopefully nothing would stand in the way. He contemplated putting a note under the door. Having it stick out just enough so you would only see it if you were looking, or if you opened the door. He didn't want some poor hotel worker to stumble upon the mess, although he had picked a method that hopefully wouldn't traumatize anyone too much. That reminded him he needed to buy some plastic sheeting to put down so he wouldn't leave too much of a mess. It was the little things that made a difference; he convinced himself. It was as considerate as he could muster, given the circumstances. The practicalities of death drifted from his mind as soon as he saw her.

As she headed over to the bar, a crowd of people walked in front of him and stood there chatting. He tried to weave his head in between them so he could get her attention, but more people started joining them, so he waited for the people to be shown to their table. Once they dispersed, he could see her sat at a small table and she had her back to him. She opened up her laptop, and he wondered if he should wait until he was on his way out before bothering her—just in case she wanted nothing to do with the pathetic mess that she had to escort to his room last night. He hopped from his table to one closer, like some crazy stalker. *What are you doing, psycho?* He noticed a familiar screen. She was calling someone over video-chat.

"Hi mom. Hi dad." He found himself strangely relieved it wasn't a boyfriend she was calling. *Now you're eavesdropping. Psycho.*

He couldn't hear what they were saying on the other end of the computer, but he could hear Olivia loud and clear.

"Listen. Calm down. It's fine. I'm fine."

He could see pixilated images of her parents. One of them was throwing their arms around as if trying to make a point.

"Yes, I'm taking precautions," she said.

It felt wrong, spying like this, and he was just about to back off to his original table when a family of four gathered around it.

"I'm doing this, whether you like it or not. There's no debate here." Her voice was loud and firm—a force to be reckoned with. "I'm not giving up on her. Not like you." She went quiet, as did her parents on the other end. Michael averted his gaze to his coffee cup, tearing on the cardboard sleeve.

"I have to know what happened." Upset and frustration bubbled up in her voice. He wondered who she was talking about and what happened to them.

The waitress approached him. "Can I get you anything else?" she asked.

"No, no. I'm fine." He mumbled, not wanting to draw attention to himself. He picked up a leaflet that had been left on the table and held it close to his face. After briefly looking at the activities on offer, he looked over at Josie again.

"I'm not naïve. Look, I know exactly what I'm doing. We're not getting anywhere. I can't keep having this same argument with you. Listen. I'm going to call you later okay. The connection is terrible." She pressed the end call button and slammed down the lid of her laptop. This was obviously a bad time and Michael decided to make himself scarce, heading for the door, not looking in her direction.

"Michael." She tapped him on the shoulder as he passed.

"Oh, Josie. Hi. I didn't see you there." He hoped he wasn't as transparent as he thought he sounded.

"Sit with me." She pulled out a chair and looked up at him pleadingly.

He stood there like an idiot for a minute as his brain tried to work out why she wanted him there. "Thanks." He dropped on to the seat. He could probably do with breakfast anyway, after losing most of last night's dinner.

He looked at the menu, trying to avoid eye contact. "I might have the huevos rancheros." Then he wondered if spicy was a good idea.

"How are you feeling?" She had the hint of a mischievous grin, like she was taking pleasure in his misfortune.

"Well, I did manage to get in eight hours of extreme anxiety with my hour of sleep, so that's a bonus. Oh, then there was the mammoth vomiting session." He regretted being so candid. He didn't want her picturing him like that.

"Ahh, poor baby." Her mouth down turned in an exaggerated frown.

"Are you pitying me, or just mocking me?" He asked, propping his sunglasses up on the top of his head.

"Hmm. Little from column A, little from column B." She flagged down the waitress and ordered herself pancakes with fruit salad, and his huevos rancheros.

"Listen, sorry I was such a mess yesterday. I'm not always on drugs, trust me."

"I was taught that when someone says trust me, it usually means they're lying."

"I… I wasn't."

"Chill, I was joking."

The Girl from Ipanema came on the radio. It was an old-fashioned song for this young crowd, but somehow it fit. "I was thinking." He got up from his chair and ran over to the other table. "Excuse me, do you mind?" He asked, reaching for the leaflet he was browsing earlier.

"Okay," said one of the girls at the table, looking overly annoyed that he had the audacity to interrupt their breakfast.

Michael sat back down and opened the pamphlet. "How about… boat trip?" For some reason he did jazz hands as he said it.

"That sounds lovely, really, but I'm leaving tomorrow and I've got a couple of things to do and…" She trailed off. For some reason, he got the impression she wanted him to talk her into it. His heart sank when she said she was leaving. He barely knew Josie, but he did know she made him feel less alone.

"Come on. Live a little. You said you're leaving. You've got to make the most of all this."

"I'm not going home. I have somewhere else I need to be."

"No, I get it." Michael wished he could leave his breakfast and let the ground swallow him whole. He had embarrassed himself enough already and this girl clearly had some heavy shit going on.

"I was thinking maybe some ruins. I've been so busy; I haven't had a chance to see any yet."

"Yeah. Totally." He smiled, and then overcompensated by frowning, not wanting to look too eager.

He flagged down the waitress. "Una cafe por favor." He assumed he had said it wrong as the waitress looked at him blankly. "Black coffee." He reverted back to English and luckily she spoke English better than he spoke Spanish.

He leaned in to Josie. "Did I say it right?"

"Your pronunciation is all off. Don't worry about it." She leaned back in her chair.

After breakfast Michael went to book the tour, and luckily there were still two seats left. He agreed to meet Josie back in the lobby. He'd seen his fair share of ruins already on this trip, but this time an odd feeling of excitement crept up on him. It had been so long, he almost forgot what it felt like.

Chapter Seven

The white bus dropped them off on the roadside, and the driver announced that they had an hour to walk around before they had to be back. There was no tour guide included, not that Michael minded, as he was far more interested in finding out what Josie had been talking to her parents about, than he was in the ruins.

Wisps of cloud stretched across the blue sky, which disappeared as they made their way into the jungle, and the trees shielded them from the constant glare of the sun. Josie stopped in front of a large sign to look at the map of the area.

"The main ruins are to the left." She took the fork in the road and he followed her down the tree-lined path. They weren't even that deep in the jungle, yet he already had two red bumps on his shoulders. Mosquitoes just loved to feast on him.

Josie watched him scratch. "Mosquitoes never seem to bite me. Like my blood isn't good enough for them."

"Think yourself lucky." He firmly rubbed his fingers across the itchy part of his arm, trying not to irritate the skin even more.

"So you never said where you're going tomorrow. Somewhere nice, I hope?"

"Arenales." She concentrated on the path ahead, marching as if she were on a mission.

"You ever heard of living in the moment? Slow down and smell the roses." He picked up his pace to keep up with her, regretting not renting one of the bikes on offer.

"I want to get to the ruins," she said, maintaining her pace.

"Life's about the journey, not the destination." He came up beside her.

"You're full of idioms today, aren't you?" She smiled.

He wondered how she wasn't all red, and out of breath like he was. It was already far more humid than it was back at the hotel. He felt sticky, like he already needed a shower since this morning. "So what's in Arenales?" He asked, trying to remain casual. "Never heard of it."

"It's not that popular. People used to go to a wildlife sanctuary near there, but it closed down a while back."

He stayed quiet, waiting for her to elaborate, hoping her words would fill the space he had left for her.

"I'm looking for something… someone."

He waited for her to finish, but no more words came. Sensing her awkwardness, he put her out of her misery. "It's fine you don't have to—"

"It was my sister. A year ago. She was kidnapped."

"Shit. I'm sorry." He had suspected she might say something like this and tried so hard to sound surprised he realized he had done a shitty job of sounding empathetic. Not that he was ever helpful in these types of situations, anyway. He didn't have anyone close enough to him to miss if they were gone.

"They never found her, not alive or de…" She couldn't finish the sentence.

"That sucks. It must be awful not knowing. Is that what you're doing in Arenales?" He swatted an insect that hovered around his face.

"I know it's stupid. I know some girl like me isn't going to get anywhere. I know I'm kidding myself. It's not like I'm going to magically find her or anything, but I can try. It's almost like… I don't know… like if I go to where she last was, that I'd be closer to her somehow."

"I understand, I mean I don't understand, obviously, but I get it." He lit up a cigarette to take the edge off, then instantly wondered if he was even allowed to smoke here. It was too late now. "Do you have a plan?" He inhaled deeply and released a stream of smoke into the air.

"Not really. When I got here, I reached out to the police, the consulate, the press. They were about as helpful as they were when it all happened."

"So what happened exactly? I mean, you don't have to tell me, but it might help to get it out, maybe?" He looked down at his cigarette as ash floated off the end.

"I was at home. I was living with my parents at the time, saving for my own place. She called. She was in a taxi and they demanded money for her release. The authorities told us not to pay, but my dad was adamant. They were supposed to let her go. My dad did everything they asked. Paid the next day to some untraceable bank account. Basically, all of their money. We wouldn't have given a shit, we would have paid anything. But they never let her go. She never came back."

Michael knew if he opened his mouth he would probably say the wrong thing. He offered her the second half of his cigarette.

"Thanks." She breathed in deeply. "I think I might look into the cab companies."

"That sounds a bit dangerous. What if something happened to you too?"

"I don't care. I've had this argument with my folks a million times already. I don't need it from someone I barely even know."

"Fine. I'll drop it." He didn't want to drop it, but he wasn't much one for confrontation.

"So, how long are you here for?" She asked, regaining composure at the flick of a switch.

"A couple of weeks." A screech made him look up at the trees, and he wondered if it was a bird or a howler monkey.

"So what are you doing here, alone?"

"I don't know. Drowning my sorrows. So what was she like?" He regretted the words as he said them, wishing he could just leave it alone.

"She was a free spirit for sure. Never home. Adventurous. Spontaneous. Reckless. Always seemed to be in some kind of trouble. I'd barely see her, I don't know if that made her disappearance harder or easier, although I couldn't imagine it being harder."

"Listen. I don't mean to intrude, or to be weird or anything, but if you get into any trouble out there, or need anything, let me know. I could always pay you a visit, check in?"

"Why don't you come? Actually. Sorry I asked. I'm sure you don't want to spend your vacation—"

"I'd like to. I would, but I spent most of my money on the hotel." It was true, but not the whole truth. He was here for a reason, a reason he couldn't be distracted from.

They stayed quiet until they reached the main pyramid. He wasn't expecting it to be so big, and it was only when he overheard other people, that he discovered this was the second largest Mayan pyramid in Mexico. Josie's eyes lit up when she saw it and she went straight to the bas of the pyramid, gazing up to the peak. There was a long white rope secured all the way up the steps for people to hold on to. It looked even steeper when he reached the first step, and vertigo already set in. He just concentrated on what was in front of him. Just one wrong step on the uneven, rugged stone and he could see himself tumbling back, cracking his head on the rock as he fell. Maybe that wouldn't be such a bad thing—just some tragic accident. He counted one hundred steps and took a deep breath before traversing the next few. The view at the top was worth it. The jungle spread as far as the eye could see, and he turned to see a look of appreciation on Josie's face.

"They say it's much worse on the way down." A sweet older lady told him in between taking photos. Maybe she had noticed how unfit he was from spending so much time planted to his couch watching television. The sounds of the forest reminded him of the nature tracks he used to listen to when he went to sleep and wanted to block out his thoughts, and a light breeze brushed past him as he tried to capture the moment in his mind like a photograph. He wanted this to be one of the last things he remembered. This random moment he was sharing with Josie, high above the trees, looking down at the world below.

By the time they had explored the other fork in the road, they still had just under an hour left. "See, this is what happens when you rush." Michael said with a hint of faux smugness.

"What are you complaining about? Now we get to relax and just take it all in." She found a shady spot for them to sit on a large tree root overlooking the smaller ruins.

"Don't judge me," he said, pulling a small bottle of rum out of his daypack.

"You've been holding out on me." She waited for him to take a swig before taking the bottle from him.

Chapter Eight

Josie wobbled as she scaled the steps to the hotel, holding her arms out as if she was walking a tightrope.

"The tables have turned," Michael said, glad not to be the one to have overindulged for a change. He felt vaguely guilty for reveling in her loss of control, but not for long.

She yanked him by the arm so hard it almost hurt, not realizing her own strength. "We should go to the bar."

"Don't you think you've had enough?" He wasn't usually one to stop a party before it had begun, but he knew she had a lot on her plate, and didn't think it would be wise for her to have a monstrous hangover the next day.

"I'm just getting started baby. You don't tell me when I've had enough. I tell you when I've had enough… when you've had enough." She grabbed his hands and clumsily moved her feet back and forth, trying to make him salsa with her at the top of the steps. Her hips swayed in such an exaggerated way, it was more comical than sexy. Michael humored her and twirled her under his arm.

"We should go dancing." Her voice echoed off the granite surfaces.

"Maybe you should eat something? Don't you have an early morning tomorrow?" Michael wanted nothing more than to dance with her until the early hours, to make the most of the time they had together, but if he knew anything, he knew that glazed look of someone that didn't know when enough was enough, as he had seen it in the mirror more times than he could remember.

"Alright mom. You know what? You're so bossy."

"People gotta look out for each other, a wise person once told me."

"Hey, you can't use my words against me. Not cool man."

"What about room service?"

"Yes, yes!" She was almost shouting. "Room service. You know what, you have the best ideas."

He decided them finishing the entire bottle of rum on the journey back had probably not been the best idea as he watched her run up to a random group of strangers by the elevator and start hugging them.

***

When the doors opened on Josie's floor, they were confronted with a large group of girls sporting light pink sashes. One woman wore a veil at such a jaunty angle it looked like it would fall off her head at any moment, only to get trampled by the procession of bachelorettes behind. A penis shaped straw hung from her mouth. Usually he couldn't imagine anything more annoying than a bachelorette party, but that night, they had caught him in a good mood.

"Wooo!!!" Josie shouted at them, which culminated in a hallway of screaming woman, and he couldn't help but laugh.

"This is me." Josie stopped in front of her door and put the keycard in. "It's not working. Why isn't it working?"

"Wrong way." Michael leaned over her, took out the card and re-inserted it the other way.

"You… you are amazing." She poked him in the chest.

"You have a pretty low bar for amazing, but I'll take it." He followed her inside, and she switched on the light, revealing clothes strewn over the floor. Somehow he had pegged her as a neat-freak.

"I'm getting daiquiris." She announced.

"Okay, but don't blame me if you end up barfing."

"I will blame only you. Nachos I'm so getting nachos." Her attention seemed to grow shorter. It was almost as if she were a caricature of a drunk person. An accumulation of every drunk stereotype going. He almost wondered if she was playing it up, until she stumbled again. He had to admit, it was fun to watch her cut loose—to see the transformation from the serious woman he had met in the elevator.

Josie sat on the bed as Michael called room service and once he had ordered their food, he scooted the armchair closer to the bed and sat down. "Can I get you a water or anything?"

"Nah I'm good." She propped herself up against the wall with a pillow behind her, and they sat quietly for a moment. As the silence went on, Josie gazed into space—her smile disappearing, replaced by a frown.

"So how are you getting to Arenales tomorrow?"

"Bus."

He considered asking her what time, so he could say goodbye to her in the morning, but something about the look on her face made him change his mind in a split second, and that was all it took to send his life hurtling in another direction. "If you still want me to, I'd like to go with you."

The smile came back to her face. "I mean yeah, if that's what you want. I'll totally cover your accommodation. I can't promise it will be as nice as here. And food and drink too. Call it payment for your services."

"My services?"

She started sliding down the wall as if she'd had enough of being vertical. "Yeah. You can be my bodyguard."

"Ha. If your idea of having me as a bodyguard is me using you as a human shield then you're on."

"You're too far away." She shifted, making space on the bed, and held her arm out to him.

Although he wanted nothing more than to join her on the bed, he thought better of it. "The food will be here any minute, I might as well—" A knock at the door came in perfect time. "I'll get it." He sprang up from his chair and walked to the door to let the steward in with his metal cart. Michael took the drinks while the steward put the plates on the table for them. "Gracias." He passed the steward a tip and brought the plates over to the bed. "Anyone order nachos?"

"Me, me. I did!" She reached out and took the plate, piled high with nachos, salsa and guacamole. "Hell yeah." She stuffed a chip in her mouth, somehow leaving salsa on her cheek in the process.

"Um, you've got a little something on…"

She grabbed another nacho and sunk it into a dollop of guacamole, dropping some onto her T-shirt. "I'm so hot right now," she said with her mouth open.

"Well, don't hog them." He reached out his hand towards the plate and she batted it away.

"My nachos." She turned away from him, shielding the plate from his grasping hands as if she wanted him to fight her for them.

He backed away. "I think I should go back to my room. I barely got any sleep last night. I'm running on fumes here."

"Well, if you're going to be a baby about it." She held out the plate to him.

He took a single nacho. "Good night. What time did you want to meet tomorrow?"

"You can't just take my nachos and leave."

He tried to work out what she wanted from him. Maybe she just didn't want to be alone. Maybe it was something else. He knew he couldn't trust himself, and he didn't want to take advantage of that dangerous mix of drunk and vulnerable. "Nachos are on me tomorrow, okay. Try to get some sleep." He put the plate on the bedside table and took a sip of his drink. "Here, you might need this." He grabbed the trash-can and placed it next to the bed.

Chapter Nine

He was half-expecting her not to be there when he got to the lobby, like the last few days had been a figment of his imagination, or some hallucination. Most of his time in Mexico had felt that way—not real. Everything looked different—everyone acted differently. Travel had its own rules. Josie stood alone as a stream of people bustled past her, rushing out the door like an ocean current. Michael had left some belongings at the hotel, as he didn't want to have a member of staff think he had gone and to give his room to someone else. He still needed that room.

It was light and airy at reception, despite crowds of people milling around waiting for their tour buses to arrive to take them where they needed to go.

He resisted the urge to creep up on her and waved to alert her of his presence. "And how are you feeling today?" he asked, approaching her slowly, as one might approach a timid wild animal.

"I've felt better. The sunglasses are helping. Tell me, why is everything so damned bright? I need to be in a dark room somewhere."

"You and me both." He followed her lead and took his shades from his pocket. He only had a hint of a hangover, but at least they could hide the dark circles under his eyes. "We can be those kinds of assholes who wear sunglasses indoors."

"So where do we get this bus from then?"

"I forked out for a private car and hotel pickup. No way am I walking anywhere today. It was hard enough getting out of bed."

"Welcome to my life." He said, seriously at first, but then forced out a laugh. No need to let her know how hard it was for him getting out of bed most mornings.

"Hola." An older looking man with white facial hair approached them. "Josie?"

"That's us." She went to grab her bag.

"Here, let me." He hoisted up her bag and slung it over one shoulder.

"I can carry my own bag," she offered, but he could tell from the slight hunch she had developed since the night before that she might just be saying that for show.

"Come on, you're sporting the hangover from hell. Don't try to be a hero."

"Okay, if you put it that way."

The driver approached them and took both bags off Michael without saying a word.

"There goes my act of chivalry." They followed the driver out the front doors and tried to match his fast pace. Even with his age and carrying two bags, he was more spritely than them. He guided them to a six-seater and put their bags in the trunk as they got inside.

"So how far is this place anyhow?"

"It's about a three-hour drive, maybe."

The engine started up and the driver put the radio and air-con on. As the car started moving, Josie lurched forward in her seat and groaned.

"You okay?"

"I feel like shit."

"I'd hate to say I told you so."

"Then don't."

"Tell me more about this place," he said, trying to distract her.

"Well, it's a village, or a small town. Close to the Belize border. A little of the beaten park, not like Tulum or Cancún. I've done some research. It has smaller Mayan ruins. Not a lot of tourists so better for exploring if you want some solitude I guess. There's a load of cenotes as well. You could swim in one all to yourself."

"Hm. I wouldn't fancy getting stuck in an underwater cave on my own." He noticed her leaning her head against the glass with a pained look on her face. "Have this." He pulled a banana from his daypack. "Potassium, that's supposed to be good for hangovers, right?" They reached the highway and Michael watched the jungle pass by as Josie slept with her head propped up against the window.

***

In and out of consciousness, Michael woke up when the car finally stopped in front of Hotel Mono Loco. A plain concrete building with a flash of green and blue paint from the logo painted on the front. Green leaves, and a badly painted monkey with one eye a lot bigger than the other. Josie was now wide awake and got out of her side of the car. It was jarring going from the lull of sleep, into the middle of some village he had never seen before. All the other buildings were small except the hotel and a nearby convenience store. A vendor sold food from their cart on the side of the road, and there were no other tourists he could see on the street. He grabbed the bags whilst Josie tipped the driver and then they headed inside. The hotel was empty except for one middle-aged traveler sat on a tattered red couch reading a magazine at the table. He felt self-conscious walking in as it was so quiet their footsteps echoed throughout the building. The front desk was unmanned, and they waited with their bags, desperate to offload their stuff. Josie picked up a card for a taxi company from the desk and looked at it with suspicion. He tried to imagine what had been running through her sister's mind when she was trapped in that taxi, alone. Worst-case scenarios running through her head—worst-case scenarios that came true. His mind couldn't help but imagine her dead in a ditch somewhere, and the thought that Josie probably also imagined these things made him feel sick.

There was some movement in the back room and a man that looked to be in his forties emerged from the office with a fine layer of sweat on his forehead. He looked surprised to see them.

"Los siento. I didn't hear you there." He sat down on a wheeled chair and scooted over to a huge beige computer that looked like it was from the late eighties and input something on the keyboard as a clunky fan droned in the background.

"Passportes por favor."

"Oh, yeah." Michael rummaged in his pocket.

"I am Julio. Anything you need, you ask." He took Josie's passport, opened it up at the photo page and held it up in front of him comparing the two. "Do I know you? You look familiar."

"No. I've never been here before." She looked confused for a brief second, and then her eyes lit up and she reached into her handbag, pulling out a photograph folded in half. She opened it and held it out to him. "Have you seen this girl at all? It may have been a long time ago now." She looked at him expectantly.

He glanced at the photo. "I don't know. I see a lot of tourists. Maybe."

Michael glanced over at the photo and couldn't believe how similar Josie and her sister were. Looking at the photo, it was like seeing into the future. It was exactly how he could imagine Josie looking if she were a few years older.

"Maybe. So you could have? Think." She pushed.

"I don't remember. Lots of beautiful girls come and go, you know. Let me show you your rooms."

They followed him up the steep concrete stairs to the first floor. "The keys are in the lock. Shared bathroom at the end of the hall, showers, hot water."

"Thank you." Josie watched him as he walked down the stairs and once he had reached the bottom, she turned to

Michael. "Did you hear that? We've been here all of ten minutes and already I have a lead. He recognized her, I know it."

"Could be. I can't believe how alike you look."

"Yeah, everyone would always say that. I might clean up and then go around town, see if anyone recognizes her. It was so long ago, I know it's a long shot. But it's a start."

Chapter Ten

Michael stood before the shelves at the convenience store, glancing over the limited range of items on sale. All the products were similar enough to give him a false sense of security, but different enough to not let him forget that he was far from home. Michael inspected a family size bag of chips, trying to decipher the flavor. Usually the pictures would give him a hint. Most of them seemed to have images of chilli's on the front, or maybe peppers. Paprika maybe. He hedged his bets—his arms laden with bags of chips and candy bars as he approached the cash register. Why were there no baskets? He dumped his stash on the side next to Josie and went down the other side of the shop in search of beer. There was barely anything left in the small refrigerator that seemed to be held together with duct tape, so he picked up some dusty bottles off of the shelf, holding them close to his chest before going back to the cash register.

"Excuse me. Have you seen this girl around at all? At any time? Could have been months ago." She slipped Tanya's photograph across the counter and leaned forward expectantly. He considered she might have more luck if she didn't get in the shopkeeper's personal space.

The young woman looked at her blankly and Josie asked her again. "Has visto a esta chica?"

The cashier took the picture from Josie, glanced at it. "Mmm, no." She shrugged, slid the photo back across the counter and started bagging up Michael's shopping in reused plastic bags.

Josie waited before she was outside the store before she spoke. "Well that was a bust. I'm going to ask the churro guy," she said, looking defeated already. Michael believed that the odds of finding out anything were slim to none, and he hoped that she had actually considered that outcome. At least she would have done everything she could, and hopefully, that would bring her some closure. They dodged a puddle from the previous night's rain and approached the street vendor.

"Hola. Puedo teines cinco churros, por favor," he said slowly, trying to enunciate every syllable. To his surprise, the vendor seemed to understand what he had said and put the sugary sticks of dough into a paper-bag. Michael's mouth was already watering, and he stood by and let Josie do her thing.

"Has visto a esta chica?" She held up the picture.

"Ha ha. Yes. She come every night. We have drinks one time. She love to party that one." A spark fired up in his eyes.

"Oh my god. Are you sure? It would have been a while ago now." She was talking with her whole body now.

"Yes. One year. I know. It was Cinco de Mayo. We party all night. Shots. Dancing. She never call me. How is she?"

"I don't know. She went missing. Desaparecida." She said, gesticulating as if she was trying to act out the word.

The man's face dropped like a man that had just found out his wife of 50 years had died. "No, no, no." He abruptly came around from his cart and gave Josie a hug. She looked stiffened up awkwardly at first, but then leaned into it.

After the hug had gone on one second too long, she pulled away. "Well we have to go. Ask around town. What is your name?"

"Ramirez." He went in for another hug. "You let me know if you find her. You're staying across the road right?"

"Yeah, I'll let you know." As Josie whisked Michael down the street she talked in a stream of consciousness. "Now I know we're onto something. He knew her. The hotel guy recognized her. I could see it in his eyes. They all seem to know her. It's crazy."

"Just don't get your hopes up." He hesitated before continuing. "Keep your expectations realistic." It only just occurred to Michael that he had left the stall without his churros despite having paid for them.

"I just feel like, if the police had done this when it happened, it would be fresh in everyone's mind, and now… it's probably too late. Well, too late or not. It won't stop me." With a straight face, and her arms swinging at her sides—she looked like a girl on a mission. "If anyone would remember her, it would be here, right?" She stopped on the corner where the two roads converged in front of a bar. **La Cocina de Maya.** "That guy said they had drinks. Maybe they had them here. I should have asked. I'm such an amateur at this."

"I'm sure he wouldn't mind if you paid him another visit." Michael tried to wink suggestively, but instead, looked like he was having a stroke.

Josie stood in front of the door to the bar. "Let's go in. I'm starving anyway, and I'm sure you could use a drink. It's already gone midday." She consulted her watch.

The light of the sun disappeared as they entered, and the other customers turned to look at them as soon as they were aware of their presence. They eventually turned their attention away and went back to cradling their drinks and chatting amongst themselves in Spanish. The smell of food and stale beer wafted around the stuffy bar. The breeze from earlier had died down, and the heat became oppressive again, like it was sucking away the oxygen from the room.

"Sit, sit. I bring you a menu." The person manning the bar was bursting with enthusiasm, his eagerness to please putting Michael at ease. "Welcome. Can I get you a drink first?"

"Could I have your finest tequila, please? And a beer." Michael couldn't decide between both, and why should he when it was so cheap.

"A man after my own heart." He held both hands in front of the left side of his chest, his every expression exaggerated. "And for the lady?" He probably wooed all his guests this way. Made them feel special.

"Just a coke, please. Extra ice."

"Coming up." He put two menus on the table and went back to the bar.

The menu was laminated and had pictures of the various dishes. "I don't know about you, but whenever a menu has photos of the food it never looks good," said Michael, perusing the greasy pages. "Potatoes with honey and mustard seeds. Weird. Sounds nice though."

"I'll probably take one of everything," she mused.

A figure emerged in the front doorway, pausing for a moment, just standing there as if waiting for everyone to notice him. He and another man walked up to the bar and the owner's relaxed stance changed as he straightened his back, standing upright like someone had a pole up his ass.

"Hola Eduardo." The man who had just walked in held his arms out as if he were a friend, but the owner, Eduardo, seemed to recoil the closer this man got and they started talking.

"Che. Que estas haciendo aqui?"

The man, Che, leaned his forearm across the bar and pulled in closer. Michael could barely make out a word except the word dinero coming up every now and then. One of the few words he knew. A word that stood out—hard to mistake for any other. Their voices got louder and Michael had that horrible feeling, like trouble was brewing. He felt strangely protective of Eduardo. He seemed warm, and instantly likable. The kind of guy you could have good times with.

"Can you understand any of this?" Michael asked, hunching over the table.

"He wants him to pay up for something, not sure what though." They both glanced at the exchange and looking down at the table periodically, not wanting to be seen paying too much attention to their private business. Something stood out about the man, but Michael wasn't sure what. Maybe it was that everyone else was dressed casually for the weather, yet this man, all in black, looked like he was ready for a funeral.

The man was actually shouting now, and Michael's blood pumped so fast around his body he could feel his pulse twitch. It was somewhere between fear and exhilaration. A secret death wish. Dying by someone else was far easier than dying by your own hand. There would be no guilt. Instead of people calling you selfish, people would mourn your loss like anyone else, babble on about how great you were at your funeral. His fantasies started as getting hit by a truck on the way to work until they escalated. Why couldn't he just get shot down in the street? A swift bullet to the brain, a terrorist attack, or an asteroid would do. Wipe out the whole sorry world in the process. Then there would be no suffering.

Eduardo escorted the two men to the kitchen to continue their business in private.

***

The two men finally reappeared from the kitchen after what felt like about half an hour and headed straight for the door, not looking back.

Eduardo watched and waited for them to go out the door before he went to pour Michael and Josie's drinks. He put them on a small circular tray along with a bowl of something and walked over to their table. "Sorry about the wait. I got you some tortilla for while you wait. On the house. Your food will be a little while."

"De nada." Josie pulled out the picture of her sister once again. "I wonder if you can help me. I'm looking for my sister. I don't suppose you recognize her at all?"

Eduardo was too busy putting the drinks on the table to give the picture a proper look, his eyes darting around, seemingly unable to stay fixed. "No. Sorry. I'll go check on your food." He hurried back to the kitchen, taking the tray with him.

Two people from the table at the other side of the bar got up and approached them. They looked to be in their mid-twenties. One of them had thick black hair swept back with a copious amount of gel—looked like he could have been a model given the right circumstances.

"Hola. Are you Americano?"

"Si." Michael replied, switching to Spanglish seemingly at will.

"Cool. What brings you here?"

Michael looked over at Josie to follow her lead. Straight away, without pretense, she pulled her sister's picture back out from her bag and passed it to them and asked that same question.

"No. Not seen her. I'm sure I'd remember if I had. Pretty girl. We live in the next town over, so that's probably why." His English sounded impeccable. "Can we get you guys a drink?" He looked at their half-finished drinks.

"No, let me." Josie reached for her purse and slipped out a note.

"I'll go." The chatty guy took her money. "No gringo prices for you. They do good rum. You'll like."

"Sorry, I didn't get your names." Josie asked the guy left at the table.

"I'm Jorge, and my friend is Álvaro."

"So what do you do?" she asked, leaning her elbows on the table and leaning her head on her hand.

"We are surgeons," he said meekly.

"Oh wow. Saving lives, eh." She finished the watered down dregs of her cola.

"Well, we haven't been doing it long. Álvaro has to do a Cesarean section tomorrow."

Josie almost spat out her drink in surprise. "Should he be drinking so much?" She looked back to see him taking a shot of rum, before picking up the tray to bring back to the table. There were enough of shots on there to bring down an elephant.

"He'll be fine. We call him La Miquina. In English that's—"

"The machine. I like it." Josie grabbed a shot as soon as Álvaro put the tray on the table. "Salud," she announced, before taking her shot and slamming the empty glass back on the table. She seemed keen. Michael wondered if this was going to be a repeat of the night before. Somehow, she'd seemed to have recovered quite well, whereas he still felt rough. Perhaps he had misjudged her, he thought as he took his shot of rum. The best way to get over a hangover was to start drinking again. He could worry about the consequences tomorrow. As the rum hit his tongue, the depth of flavor surprised him—sweet, aromatic, and complex, with a hint of something spicy.

"Honey rum. Good, no?" Álvaro nodded in encouragement and picked up two shots and passed them to Michael and Josie. "We don't see so many tourists these days," Álvaro made it so his and Josie's chairs were touching.

"And why is that?" He had piqued her interest.

"It can be dangerous."

"Like what kind of dangerous are we talking? Mugging? Kidnapping?"

"Things are changing. Places used to be safer y'know. Tulum, Cancún, Acapulco. Tourists are a lot less off limits than they used to be. It wasn't worth the hassle. The media shit-storm. These new gangs. They don't care. The cartels broke up into so many different gangs y'know. Now it's just one big cluster-fuck. This place, no one cares. People do what they want. Not to scare you, but just stay alert, y'know."

"Yes. Of course." Josie straightened up. She had let herself get too comfortable.

"Where are you staying anyway?"

"Mono Loco, just down the road."

Michael wondered if she should be giving them the name of where they were staying. He got good vibes from them, but why take the risk?

"You'll be safe there. Julio always pays on time. Very agreeable."

"Pays for what?" asked Michael.

"Protection. Some of the people, the businesses, are still resistant y'know. It's not worth it. Just take the hit."

"What do you know about the taxi companies here? Are they safe?" Josie probed.

"There is only one. It's safe, so far as I know. You should be able to take taxi, no problem."

"Well, thanks for letting us know. We should be getting back to the hotel." Michael looked around for Eduardo, but he must have disappeared out back.

Álvaro waved his arms in protest. "No, we're just getting started."

"Michael's right. We got barely any sleep last night."

"Oh." He looked surprised and contemplative, like he was working out if they were a couple or not, but then deciding he didn't care. "But your food is just coming."

"I don't know. I feel so tired. It's really hitting me now." Josie scanned the room for Eduardo.

"Okay. Eduardo," he shouted. "These guys want their food to go. See. No point wasting good food. I can walk you back to the hotel."

"It's not even dark yet. We'll be fine," She looked back at the kitchen.

Álvaro's lips turned up slightly in a strange grin. "Why the hurry?"

Josie changed the subject and started talking about things to do in the area until Eduardo emerged from behind the bar and walked over with two cardboard takeout boxes. "Enjoy."

Josie gave the money straight to Eduardo. "Keep the change." She grabbed the boxes and stood upright.

"Let's go then." Álvaro gave his friend a nod, and they had a shot of rum each before getting up, leaving the rest of the rum on the table.

"Adios Eduardo." Michael called across the bar, and they headed for the exit. A warm current of air whooshed in as they opened the door. The once light, clear sky outside now drained of color as a thick gray shelf cloud loomed overhead, blocking out the sun, making it look much later than it was. Murky brown water still sat, stagnant in potholes from the last downpour.

"There's a storm coming," said Jorge, looking up. He had been so quiet all night that it was almost jarring to hear him speak. He could see his face better outside, and committed it to memory. His left cheek was dented with acne scars, but somehow, it worked for him. They crossed the road. "So what do you do for the rest of your trip?" he asked as he put his hands in his pockets.

"Not sure yet." Michael looked around. The main street was devoid of people and looked like something from a western as grit from the road was kicked up in the air by the wind. He almost expected to see a pair of old-wooden saloon doors. As they got further down the road, Michael spotted

Ramirez at his cart. He felt sorry for the guy, he couldn't have much business. He waved at him from the other end of the street. A motorcycle's buzzing engine tore through the silence as it whizzed past, kicking up more dust in its wake.

"This is us," Josie said, preparing to cross the road. Looking both ways, despite how quiet it was.

"Nice to meet you. If you need anything, let us know. Give me your phone."

"What?"

"I'll put my number in. You need anything, give us a call."

"Oh, yeah. Sure." Josie slid her phone out of her pocket and unlocked it for Álvaro to input his number, seemingly unfazed. What could it hurt Michael decided, and he took his details as well.

"Good luck on the surgery tomorrow," said Michael.

"What?" Álvaro said, looking up from the phone.

"Jorge said you are performing a C-section tomorrow."

"Ah, yes." He turned to Jorge. "We should go home." They headed back to the restaurant in a hurry, leaving Michael and Josie stood on the sidewalk looking at each other with an uneasy look that turned into a smile."

"Well that was… something." Michael laughed.

Chapter Eleven

There was something about standing in front of a mirror and brushing his teeth that always sent Michael into a trance. It could quite possibly have been the only time when his mind wasn't in overdrive. His mouth hung open as he rhythmically rotated the brush across his teeth. A dog barking from outside ruined the peaceful moment and Michael spat into the sink before looking at the man staring back at him in the mirror. Pallid skin, Tired. No matter how much time he spent in the sun, he could never quite get a tan, or even the hint of a healthy glow.

A selection of T-shirts lay strewn on the bed, so he did the sniff test, deeming which ones he could wear again, and tossing the rest in the corner before heading to Josie's room. He knocked gently and waited on the landing, listening for signs of life. Nothing. He rapped louder on the door. Maybe she was out on the streets already, showing Tanya's photo around.

As he plodded downstairs that same person sat on the couch from when he first checked in and he wondered if they ever left that spot. Julio sat behind the front desk on his phone until he noticed Michael. "Breakfast is in the kitchen still." He called. "Normally I clear everything away at ten, but thought you might need some food. Late riser, huh?"

"Thank you." Michael didn't even know the hotel had a kitchen and walked past the front desk to a dim corridor. There was a dorm room on each side with rickety wooden bunk beds, but no guests. Only one bed had a bag on it to signal it was taken. He made a mental note as he walked past a small utility room with a washing machine that it was definitely time to tackle some laundry.

At the bottom of the corridor to his left, Josie navigated a cramped room. There was a microwave caked in dry splatters of red and brown, a small burner, and a sink stacked high with mismatched kitchenware. It looked like a giant game of Jenga, and the pile was about to collapse any minute. A string of shriveled, dry chilies hung from a hook on the wall that looked like they could have been there for centuries.

Josie grabbed a slice of bread, dropping crumbs on the side, and spread a thick layer of peanut butter and jelly onto it before dropping it onto a flimsy plastic plate. "Afternoon," she said, licking a stray piece of peanut butter off of her finger.

"Hey there. I thought you'd left without me. So what's the plan today?"

It wasn't until he saw the jug of apple and orange juice that he realized how thirsty he was. He went for one of each, taking a small plastic cup from the side.

"I found out where the taxi company office is. There is only one company operating here, so shouldn't take long. Then I thought we could do something nice. Get out of here for a bit."

"Sounds good."

"You're not eating?"

"I had our leftovers late last night. Not really hungry yet. I still have a stockpile of Cheetos in the room."

"So healthy. Here. I refuse to let you live off the dream diet of an eight-year-old." She passed him an apple.

"It's not like your breakfast is the epitome of health. You have any idea how much sugar is in that jelly… and the white bread?"

"Quit whining and eat. We have work to do." She tore her sandwich in half and shoveled half of it down, barely chewing.

"So did she describe the taxi at all, when your dad spoke to her?"

"Not really. The police said it would be almost impossible to trace. Apparently there are loads of unlicensed drivers operating in the area."

"It's scary. All it takes is being in the wrong place at the wrong time."

"She shouldn't have got in there alone." Josie muttered, clutching a mug of coffee as she stared into the distance.

Chapter Twelve

The small grey concrete building looked more like an auto-repair than a taxi company. A metal rack full of car parts ran across one side of the garage and three yellow and white taxis sat parked in the lot. The reek of diesel made Michael feel a little light-headed.

There was a small office for tourists to book trips and car services. A short-stocky man, spilling out of his jeans, stepped out before they could even make it inside. "Taxi?" he asked, rubbing excess motor oil off his hands onto his white t-shirt.

Josie went through her routine and showed him the picture of Tanya, and the man glanced at it for a split second, a look of disinterest on his face. Josie then pulled out another slip of paper. A partial license plate number. "You have any cars with this plate? Placa." The man shrugged at her. "Do you have records? Registro's?"

He waved her off as if she were an annoying insect, turning to go back inside.

"I pay." She reached for her wallet, but the man walked straight back into the building. She stood there and Michael could almost see the inner workings of her brain through her eyes. Chugging away, thinking of next steps. A cab pulled up next door, and she went straight over to it before the driver even had time to park up. She went straight into Spanish and Michael took a step back. He felt like an extra limb, surplus to requirements, and stood aimlessly while Josie did her thing, a part of him wondering how the hell he had ended up here. What the hell was he doing?

"Well, that was a bust," Josie said, walking past him. He followed her out and watched as she paced the sidewalk.

"So what now?"

***

They sat in the hotel communal area, Josie's laptop open on the table. "This Wi-Fi sucks." She mashed the keys out of frustration.

"Why don't you tell me more about yourself? I feel like I know more about your sister than I do about you." He twirled a loose thread of fabric on the couch, incapable of keeping his hands still.

"That sounds about right."

"What do you mean?" He straightened up from his slouched position.

"It's not easy being the younger one. Everyone says that parents dote on the younger sibling. I call bullshit." She pounded the keyboard with her fist now, and he could picture her throwing the thing across the room.

"I think I would have liked having a brother or sister."

"The grass is always greener. Sorry. I don't know why I said that. She was awesome. Life of the party. She always did everything before I did though. By the time I achieved anything, she had always gotten there first. I kinda double corrected. Perfect grades, studied my ass off, never got in trouble, but for some reason my parents didn't seem to give a shit. They were always more concerned with her. There was always some drama. I always got so mad at her for it, but now, now I'd kill to have her call with her latest crisis. One time, I remember, she ran out of money in Australia. Hitchhiked. Ended up staying with some random middle-aged dude in Cairns. For some reason, she felt compelled to tell our parent's all the gory details. Man, they were pissed."

Michael forced out a laugh to detract from the fact that he would have given his right arm to have someone give a shit about him.

"Anyway, you're one to talk. I know next to nothing about you. It's funny that isn't it? I've never really traveled outside of the states. I've worked with people for years and barely talk to them, yet I've known you a few days and I already feel like…"

"I know what you mean. Trust me though, there's nothing to tell. My life is the least interesting story in history."

"Yes!" Josie declared as her laptop sprung to life. "Come over here,"

"What?" He mustered the energy to get his body off of the sofa.

"I finally got into her account. I've been trying to guess her password for the last year. There has to be something." She scrolled through reams of messages, writing down the names of anyone she had conversed with before she disappeared. She sent a group message from her own profile begging for information. Any snippet, no matter how insignificant. While she waited to see if anyone would respond, she scrolled through all her photographs again.

The pictures showed a story. One edited and filtered until you could no longer be sure it resembled reality. Choreographed to show a perfect life. She was surrounded by groups of people, all beaming smiles and flattering camera angles. No pictures of a girl scared and alone, on dark streets, trapped in a cab and driven to her fate. He could barely imagine that grinning face with a look of terror on it, what those eyes might look like as she tried to escape. They identified where she was from tags, and landmarks. They scoured the Internet to find which ruins she was posed in front of, which stretch of sea she was lounging on, which bars she was drinking at. The second to last picture they recognized was the next street across from them, but the very last photo didn't seem to fit with the one that came before. It was somewhere different. She stood in front of a white tower. It looked like a cross between a lighthouse or a small signal tower that you might see in an airport.

"What's that?" Michael asked.

"Not sure. Is that sea in the background?" Josie traced her finger along a fuzzy stretch of blue behind a white wall. "Looks like it."

"I'm going to ask." She picked up her laptop and walked over to Julio, who sat, unmoved from his position at the front desk. "Can I ask, do you recognize this place? We want to go." She placed her computer on the side and rotated it to face in his direction.

He leaned over the desk and squinted at the laptop. "Yes. Chetumal. Nice place. You can learn to dive. Go sailing. I have boat there."

"Is it easy to get there from here?"

"Very easy. You can get taxi, or I can even drive. Give you a tour. My nephew can always watch this place."

"That's amazing, thanks." Josie rushed back to Michael. "Did you hear that? Chetumal. We can get a cab. It will give me a chance to take another crack at the taxi driver too. Ask them some questions. Captive audience and all." He watched Josie type Chetumal white tower into her search engine and pour through the images with a newfound vigor. "This is it." She pointed at the tower she had seen Tanya posing in front of. Her leg shook as she tapped her foot against the floor. "We should go now. It's still early." He watched her range of emotions swirling into one rotating vortex of energy.

"Josie, Michael," Julio called from the front desk. He had his phone still in his hand. "My nephew will watch the hotel now. I can take you if you like? Show you Chetumal?"

"Are you sure?" Josie asked, a huge grin on her face.

"As soon as Frederico gets here we go."

"I'm going to put my laptop away." She raced upstairs, leaving Michael stood there in her wake.

"Hang on." He headed after her.

***

"What the hell is happening right now?" He leaned against the wall as she placed her laptop in a large metal locker, shut the door with a clunk, and turned the key.

"What if this wasn't the last place she was? She was in this Chetumal place. We were talking to the wrong taxi company the whole time. I have a good feeling about this."

"But going with this guy. You think that's a good idea?"

"What, our hotel owner? Don't you think you're being a bit paranoid?"

"It wouldn't hurt to be cautious."

"Here would this make you feel better?" She passed him her phone. A post uploaded to her profile, tagging them both at the hotel and informing everyone they were traveling to Chetumal. "Everyone knows where we are, and Julio knows it. Let's go."

Chapter Thirteen

They walked around the back of the hotel to Julio's car. A beat up old Chevy that looked like it had been in a few collisions in its time. Most of the rear wheel-arch dented inward, so the jagged metal almost touched the tire. He still had trouble with the fact that Julio was so happy to just drop everything to take them there, not that the hotel was busy—it could probably take care of itself. Despite this newfound information, Michael was still convinced that Josie would be going home none the wiser. Life rarely gave endings wrapped up in neat packages. As he opened the door and stepped into the back seat, he moved aside the junk-food wrappers and discarded liquor bottles that littered the back of the car. As Michael tried to pull his seat belt forward, it jammed in one place and wouldn't pull out any further, so he gave up on it, letting it retract back where it came from.

***

Michael started to feel more at home as they drove into Chetumal —a port city bordering Belize. The small dive shops and palm trees dotted along the coast gave the place a Caribbean feel, and the many bars and restaurants catering to tourists gave him the urge to knock back a cold one. He couldn't help but wonder why Julio wouldn't have a hotel here instead and assumed it must be a lot more expensive to buy property here.

Julio pointed out various landmarks and suggested the two of them go to see manatees in the nearby mangrove shores. He then pointed out his cousin's house on the left and Michael smiled and nodded. Josie perched on the edge of her seat with her face close to the window, taking in every little detail. Julio went onto explain how the various hurricanes that had hit the shores over the last few years destroyed most of the remaining old wooden clap-board houses, which were now replaced with concrete.

"There it is." Josie craned her neck out of the back window and pointed over at the tall white lighthouse. "Can we stop?" she asked.

"Okay, but quickly. I want to take you on the boat, but don't want to set off to late," Julio said, and as soon as he slowed the car Josie jumped out, before he even had time to park up. He used the side-walk as a temporary parking space but stayed in the car. "Michael. Tell her to be quick. It's a museum now. You know." Michael was unsure how the tiny white box of a building attached to the lighthouse could be a whole museum. Instead of going inside, he waited outside and took in the sun.

***

After the museum had yielded no results, Julio drove them back in the direction of the port. Near to the main dock where the larger ships left from was a private port where Julio's boat was situated. Julio parked up in front of the main arched entranceway and led them down a set of concrete steps. They followed a gangway to the wooden pier that stretched into the sea, and their footsteps sounded like a drumbeat against the wooden planks. Two rows of large boats and small white yachts swayed on the water, tethered to their moorings. Michael watched with interest as Julio jumped onboard the boat and started up the engine, wondering how Julio could afford a yacht, yet his hotel was like a ghost-town.

"What are you waiting for? Get on." Julio swung his arms, gesturing at them to jump onboard.

Josie stepped over the side of the boat and waited for Michael to join her.

"Sit, sit," said Julio, and as he climbed up on the side of the yacht, untying the bowline from the mooring, the boat started pulling away from the dock. Some people found the unnatural movement on water made them sea-sick, but it soothed Michael. The gentle side to side was comforting, maybe it harkened back to being a baby and being rocked in his crib, not that he remembered that, but he could imagine his mother sat over him, singing some sort of lullaby, back when she was alive.

Julio reached into a white cooler at the front of the boat and pulled out three bottles of beer that had probably been sat out in the sun for days. Still, Michael wasn't complaining. "Let's get this started." He smiled and continued steering. "Enjoy. We should see Belize soon across the water."

"Thank you." Michael said, pulling off the twist top of his beer. It was lukewarm, but this didn't phase him. As they got further away from the dock, the smell of boat-diesel dissipated, leaving the fresh salty sea.

Josie looked hesitant before she spoke. "So is there much crime here?"

"Chetumal is very safe. You're safe here." Julio looked in his element playing sailor, and they continued cruising along the calm water. Green strips of land flanked them in the distance, and the sky above was almost a perfect canvas of powder-blue with a smattering of feathery clouds. The boat started rocking with more gusto as they picked up speed and got further out. The water got a little more turbulent, but was still relatively calm. After they had sailed for around 30 minutes Julio stopped the engine. Michael hadn't realized how loud the engine had been until Julio switched it off and they were just left with the sound of lapping water. It was like a different world on the sea. All the bull-shit of land left behind, and now they were just surrounded by sea, sun and sky. This is what Michael had had in mind, how he'd wanted to spend his last few days. Only now he got to share it with Josie. Not that she could appreciate it. He could sense it on her, the weight. Every now and then it would leave her, like when they danced on the hotel steps in Tulum. He hoped, whatever this trip brought, that she could let go, if even just a little. There are things in this life that you cannot control, and the more you fixate on them, the more they control you.

Chapter Fourteen

"I think I'm going to go back to asking random people on the street," Josie said, idly shuffling a pack of cards against the table back at La Cocina de Maya in Arelanes. Somehow the clear skies of earlier were long gone. A dark cloud permanently hung over Arenales like it didn't deserve the light. "I don't know what was going through my head, really. Like what did I think was going to happen? I would come here, ask a couple of questions and somehow manage to find someone the police couldn't find, with all their resources. My parents were right. What a joke." She tossed the pack of cards to one side and slumped on the table.

"Back at the hotel. You said that coming to the last place she was would make you feel closer to her. Has it?"

"You know what, it kind of has. You know how twins say stuff like, 'oh I feel the other one's pain,' and stuff like that. I kind of get it. It's like a feeling. A sixth sense, maybe. I know that sounds ridiculous."

"Well, I wouldn't know. Only child here."

"You know what they say about only children, right?" Josie's smile re-emerged.

"No, enlighten me."

"That they're weirdos."

"You got me." He raised his hands in submission before taking a sip of beer—cold this time. "Today was weird, don't you think? My brain was like, you are so going to be dumped in the ocean, sleeping with the fishes. Don't know why. I think you've made me paranoid."

"I had the weirdest dream last night. Tanya was in it. I was wandering through the desert and I swear I could see her in the distance. So I hurried, and hurried, but I could never catch up to her."

"Strange. Maybe it was a premonition."

"I doubt it, I then found a Bugatti Chiron and started cruising through the desert."

"Nice." Michael considered asking Eduardo for another drink, but got the feeling Josie was keen to go. "Shall we go interrogate some people then? You can be bad cop, I'll play good cop."

"Why do I have to be bad cop?"

"You're better at it then me. I could just see you waterboarding someone."

"Holy shit. When did we get on to torture?"

"Come on. We should go ask around before it gets dark." He put some money on the table and they walked out together.

The clouds swirled in the air, coming together into one dark formation as they walked in the opposite direction to the hotel. As always, it was extremely quiet. Quiet enough to make them feel conspicuous. The first person they came across was a local woman hanging up washing out the front of her house. Josie honed straight in like a homing missile, and he was impressed with her confidence to approach anyone. Again Michael stood on the sidelines with nothing to offer. At first the lady looked disinterested, concentrating on her washing, but as Josie continued, the woman put her basket down and got closer. As they stood face-to-face, Michael started paying attention to what they were saying as the woman switched from Spanish to English.

"There is nothing for you here. You should go back home. Don't think they don't know you're here. They know. They know everything that goes on here."

Michael came up alongside Josie as A man came out of the house carrying a child in his arms, looking them up and down.

"Maria. Vuelve adentro."

As the lady went to go back inside Josie raised her voice. "Who knows? Who's they? Quien?" The woman didn't turn back, and the man looked up and down the street before closing the door behind her.

"Oh my god Michael. Did you hear that? I can't believe it. I'm on to something."

He didn't know what to think. All he knew was his stomach felt like a lead weight. "It could mean anything. Maybe they just don't want you stirring up trouble. Didn't that scare you?"

"Scare me? This is what I've been waiting for, I'm fucking ecstatic."

"Okay. Well, where do we go from here?"

"Let's carry on this way." She continued down the path, looking back, waiting for him to follow her. Her hair swayed behind her as the wind picked up.

As they got to the outskirts of the village, they stopped at the dirt road lined with dogwood trees, to decide which direction to turn. The trees seemed more full of life than the village, birdsong, the chirps of insects, reminding Michael of the particularly itchy mosquito bite on the side of his arm.

"There's not much up here. We should probably turn back."

"It won't be dark for a couple of hours, might as well make the most of it."

"If we go left, then do a loop, maybe. I can't see anything up there," she said, squinting as she looked up the path to their right. Stony dirt scrapped under their shoes as they clung close to the side of the road. A break in the clouds revealed their shadows, which stretched down the road. There was no pavement, not that there were any cars around to make way for. Most of the dilapidated houses looked abandoned, overgrown with plants, graffiti on the walls. Gray concrete against the natural browns and greens. A small store sat, abandoned on the corner on their left-hand side, sun-bleached red paint now orange, bars on the window and a faded Cristal logo on the wall. At the end of the next block, two local teenagers sat slumped against the wall.

"Hola," she said as she approached them. If anyone was going to talk to them, it would be these two. Flopped out on the pavement, grinning like idiots. Michael tried to recall if he was even carefree at that age. As they turned to look at Josie, they raised themselves up from the floor. Their faces changed in a micro-second. Something had put the fear of god into them. The pair ran, taking off around the corner.

Chapter Fifteen

"Josie!" Michael grabbed her by the arm and yanked her in the direction of the alley in front of them."What?" she cried with surprise as she got dragged along. She glanced back and saw him, dressed in black, marching towards them with purpose. He reached behind his back and they dived into the alley, weaving past a streetlight that leaned to one side. Josie scream and a cracking sound pierced Michael's eardrums.

He was incapable of making a sound now, except panting as he ran. The wall next to them splintered as the brick obliterated into an explosion of powder. His ears rang as the blood pounded around his head. Gravel shot up near his feet as another shot fired. They turned the corner. Michael had never run for his life before. Surprised at how fast his body could take him. Sprinting so quickly, lactic acid already built up in his legs and they tried to drag him down.

The wall to their right was short. If they had a few seconds, they could probably scale it and put a few inches of concrete between them and him. A split second decision, there wasn't time. They turned to the left. If they did a loop, maybe they could get back to the hotel. Would they even be safe there? His heart and lungs pounded and burned in his chest, and he wondered how long he could keep up this pace. He daren't look back, as there was no time.

Back on the main street, they clung close to the walls as they ran. Barely able to breathe, Michael ducked behind a large stone building, shielded by the wall for a few seconds. They stood in front of a small dull-yellow house set back from the rest. Michael put his foot on the crumbing front wall and levered himself up to the roof with an unstable rusty pipe and helped Josie up the way he had come, pulling her up by her arm and onto the concrete roof. From the top of the house he could see telegraph wires, palm trees and the other rooftops.

They climbed up onto the roof of the house next door, only slightly higher than the one they were standing on. Rough debris and rocks grazed his knees as he scrambled up. They looked down the other side to see a row of small gardens between the parallel lines of houses. If they lowered themselves down into one of the gardens, they might end up trapped.

"We should jump over." Michael wasn't even aware if this guy was still on their tail any more or if he had ran off. All he knew is he didn't want to wait around to find out. "We can jump over."

"No way we can make that," She panted as she knelt down to catch her breath, chest heaving.

They found a break in the gardens and walked across the roof of one of the larger buildings that joined the two rows. The street with their hotel on devoid of people. The guy could be anywhere now.

"The hotel is really close. We should just make a run for it," Josie said as her eyes scanned the street below.

"Agreed." Michael prepared to drop to the ground.

***

As they rushed through the front door, Julio looked up from his phone. They both spoke over each other at the same time, incomprehensible and panicked. Michael tried to get a hold of himself, to make sense, and the harder he tried, the harder he failed.

"Policia!" Josie demanded. One simple word that got their point across.

Julio stood up from his chair, a look of confusion, or maybe hesitation.

"Police. We got shot at." She stomped to the front desk and reached for the phone. Julio snatched the phone away before she could pick up the receiver, so she grabbed her cellphone from her pocket.

"No," he said. "I take you. We must get away from here. Come."

Josie and Michael looked at each other. Were they going to go with him? All they knew was they wanted to get as far away as possible. "Come. I will explain." He held his car keys in his hand and ushered them out of the door. They ran around the back of the hotel to Julio's Chevy. They got in the back and Julio started up the engine, taking off in a hurry.

"Do you know what's going on?" Josie asked as she looked out the back window for any sign of the shooter.

"I can take you to police, but not a good idea." He cruised along, not stopping at the intersection.

"Why not? Do you know who tried to kill us? Is it to do with my sister?" She banded out questions faster than Julio could answer them.

"The police will do nothing; it is not in their interests to go against him."

"Against who?"

"Listen, I don't know about your sister, but you've pissed someone off."

"Him. You said him. Can you take us to the police station? I want this on the record. In case something happens."

"Okay. I take you."

Josie stopped with the stream of questions and sat in silence, deep in thought. Michael wondered yet again what they had gotten themselves into. Before agreeing to help her, he thought the biggest danger they would probably face would be getting mugged or something. Ultimately, he had pictured her leaving the country alive, but had no idea what to think now. He was due to take his pentobarbital in just a few days. The bottle was still in a locker in the hotel reception. He supposed he could always buy more if his bag were to be stolen, or if he was unable to return to the hotel for it. No matter how out of hand things got here—he would make it back to Tulum—he had to.

The thought of going to the police did not appeal to him; he would rather hightail it out of there and be done with the whole thing, but there was no way Josie was going to let it go, not now. They were clear of Arenales and on a main road. Maybe they were safe now; maybe not. Michael had no idea how long it was to the next town, but assumed that was where Julio was taking them. They took an exit off of the main highway along a two lane road with trees running along each side and the odd car speeding past them.

Josie fumbled with her phone, and he looked over to see what she was doing. She loaded up a GPS application and honed in on where they were.

"How far is the police station?" Michael asked. Josie ignored him and leaned forward.

"Julio, why are we going this way? We should have stayed on Carre Merida, shouldn't we?"

A switch went off in Michael's mind as soon as he heard the click of the child-locks being activated. Before Josie even knew what was happening, Julio reached into the back and grabbed the cell phone straight from her hand. "Yours too," he demanded, glaring at Michael before pulling into a dirt layby. Josie yanked at the door handle as Michael reached into his pocket.

"It's not here. I must have dropped it when that man chased us."

"Bullshit." Julio's change of demeanor shocked Michael so he could barely hold a thought in his head as he tried to remember where he last had it.

"It's not here. I swear," he stuttered in time with his racing heartbeat.

Josie was still struggling to open the door despite it not opening on her last few attempts—the definition of insanity.

"Stop." Julio's voice blasted like a deafening siren as he reached into the glove compartment, pulling out a gun. Michael knew fuck all about guns. He'd briefly considered it as a suicide option, but after an afternoon spent looking at photographs and videos of gunshot victims on the Internet, he had decided against it. The mess they left behind was not like the movies, a neat hole. He'd seen waterfalls of blood, crushed, distorted faces that didn't resemble humans anymore. The backs of exploded heads from the exit wounds. Skull fragments. Brain fragments. He didn't want anyone finding him like that.

He looked Michael up and down, sizing him up. "If you lie to me, I shoot your girlfriend straight in the head. You hear me?" He started the car back up, kicking up dust as he turned back onto the road.

"Where are you taking us?" Josie asked. Michael wished she would keep her mouth shut. He didn't want this guy angered anymore than he was already. Maybe if they sat quietly—they could think—formulate a plan. Julio didn't respond to her anyway and kept his eyes on the road ahead.

Michael didn't know whether to look at her or not, whether Julio would decide they were colluding and pop a bullet in their heads. He took the risk and looked up from the floor just long enough to shoot her a glance. He had expected her to look as scared as he was, but if anything, she had a fire in her eyes, a fury waiting to be unleashed at the first available opportunity. She took his hand firmly, interlocking her fingers with his as if telling him with certainty that everything was going to be fine.

Perhaps together they could overpower him, make him lose control of the car, get the gun off of him, climb over and get out the front. Too many ifs and buts, all they could do was bide their time. See whoever he was taking them too, reason with them. He got the impression that all she wanted was the truth, at whatever cost. The truth was worth dying for to her, and he was okay with that. The light changed as the orange hues of sunset formed in the sky ahead. If it weren't for the circumstances, it would have been beautiful.

As a car came towards them from the horizon, Josie pulled her hand away from his and pressed up against the window. As it got closer, he could see black and white. It was a police car. He concentrated on it as if willing it to stop with the power of his mind, yet convinced it would just drive past. It was slowing. The car's lights flashed, indicating Julio to stop and Julio complied. He wound down the window and started talking to them. If only Michael could understand what they were saying. He looked over at Josie again. Should they say something? They had to fight, and this was there one and only chance. The gun rested in the right-hand side of his waist-band, invisible to the cop, but within reaching distance for Michael—it's as if Julio knew Michael didn't have the balls to take it and left it there, taunting him. Michael had no doubt Josie would have. Maybe that was Michael's problem. He was incapable of taking control of any situation, especially his own life. Julio reached for the glove-box and pulled out some papers and passed them out the open window. As the police officer glanced over the documents, Julio slipped the gun from his side, and before Michael could speak, could form a thought, Julio raised the gun up and pulled the trigger. The officer dropped to the ground in a second and flecks of blood sprayed against the window. Julio had not hesitated in shooting a cop, they didn't stand a chance.

Chapter Sixteen

"You don't move." He opened his door, waving his gun at them, before sliding out. Despite his lack of physical fitness, he had no trouble pulling the body around the front of the car, and dragging it into the bushes. A line of blood followed behind on the gravel like a slug trail.

While Julio was distracted, Josie leaned down and pulled an empty rum bottle from the floor that was wedged under the driver's seat in front, and held it down at her side. The door slammed as Julio jumped back into the car and pulled away with a screech. There was no way she could get a good angle to strike him from the back seat with the headrest up so high, so she waited. Every second on the road felt like an hour, and no-one dared speak. The car slowed as Julio started applying the breaks and turned into a side road overtaken with trees. Branches and leaves slapped against the windows as he weaved erratically over bumps in the road. If anyone was going to be executed, this would be the place to do it.

Shielded from the main road, under the cover of forest and the impending darkness. Michael wondered what was waiting for them at the end of the road, and then he got his answer. The overgrown foliage gave way to a clearing, a small mossy hut with a rusty brown corrugated iron roof looked like it hadn't seen human interaction for years. They couldn't go like this, to disappear like Josie's sister, posing more unanswerable questions. The car came to a stop. The child-locks clicked open.

"Get out!"

Michael got out as quickly as he could, stumbling as he stepped onto the uneven ground, and shut the car door behind him, a tinny sound sending reverberations into the forest. He rushed to the front of the car. The damp earth beneath his feet released a musty smell with every step. "Hey. Slowly." Julio didn't take his eyes off Michael. In the dwindling light his brown eyes were almost black, like looking down a dark well with no end. Michael heard Josie's car door close. "What is going on?" Michael shouted, trying to hold Julio's attention. As Josie came up behind, Julio span around just in time for the bottle to make contact with his forehead. A hollow thud, and a crack. Julio stumbled backwards, dropping his gun, but remained upright. The bottle remained intact in Josie's hand and as she lurched forward and swung it at Julio again, he grabbed her wrist and wrenched her arm down, sending the bottle rolling across the dried leaf-litter on the ground and under the car. As Michael's brain finally kicked into gear, he ran at them, grabbing Julio from behind, his arm around his thick neck. Julio tried to throw him off, flailing like a bucking-bronco, and smashed Michael backwards against a tree, knocking the wind out of him.

Michael could just about make out Josie, scrabbling around amongst the leaves to find the gun. Julio turned around and lunged at him again. Michael dodged to his right and grabbed Julio's head, ramming it into the trunk of the tree, using Julio's own momentum against him. The sound of skull slamming against bark. He watched in disbelief as Julio collapsed at the base of the tree. His body had worked independently of his mind, an out-of-body experience. He wasn't capable of these things. His hands trembled.

"Is he?"

"Unconscious? Dead? I don't know." He couldn't bring himself to check. He had to dissociate himself from the heap on the floor.

Josie didn't waste any time before crouching down to have a look, but she wasn't checking for signs of life. She rifled through his pockets. Her cell phone was in his pocket and she took it back, before digging deeper into his pocket, and then checking the other. "Where are they?"

"What?"

"The car keys," she yelled impatiently. "Check in the car."

Michael opened the door of the unlocked car, checking the ignition and the front seat. Nothing. "The keys must be on him."

"They're not. I've checked every pocket." She took her attention away from Julio and ran her hands through the debris on the floor.

"Josie, this is like looking for a needle in a haystack. We're just going to have to go by foot."

"Are you kidding?"

"Let's get out of here." Michael started back up the path they had come from. "Josie, come on!" She finally tore herself away from searching for the car-keys and they sprinted back down the road they had come from. There were no cars on the road, no headlights to illuminate the way. Just shadows and darkness.

"We better not stick to the main road. If he wakes up." Michael didn't want to finish his sentence.

"I think we're better off taking are chances in the forest, at least we'll have cover, plenty of places to hide." She walked across the road and shone the dim light of her phone into the bushes on the other side.

"Should we phone the police?"

"I just need some time to think first. Besides, we're not going to be safe waiting here for them, not if Julio wakes up. Remember what Álvaro said—about the police being in their pockets."

"If that was the case, why did Julio kill that cop?"

"Fuck it, let's just keep moving."

Chapter Seventeen

The dense forest left them just enough room to weave between the obstacle course of trees and bushes of ferns that clawed at their legs as they walked. Roots curled in and out of the earth, and they cursed every time they stumbled on one. It was almost pitch-black and Michael's legs ached from each and every considered step he took. The trees closed in on them, almost impenetrable, suffocating. Michael's skin crept with claustrophobia, and he regretted straying too far from the road as invisible insects tickled his skin, making his hairs stand on end. They swerved to their right, where the forest was less thick and held out their arms in front of them, feeling their way through the never-ending maze.

"This will be quite the story to tell when you get home." Michael tried to air on the side of optimism, for once. He slapped his left arm. That was definitely a bug.

"After this." Josie paused as she ducked under a vine. "You're so going to have to come visit me. You're stuck with me now, Michael."

He recognized that voice. The one full of wavering uncertainty, yet the words told a different story. The voice that says your fine when someone asks, the voice that is anything but fine. It was almost unnoticeable at first—until it wasn't. Michael could step unimpeded. The trees started becoming more and more spaced out. The thick carpet of plants that lined the forest floor thinned until there was just dirt under his feet. It was only when Josie turned the display on her phone on that the path revealed itself to them. Michael stopped and sighed with relief.

"We're still in the middle of nowhere." She looked around to decide which direction to head. "Do you think the police could tell where we are from tracking my cell, because I have no idea." She held her phone up to the sky, checking the signal bar.

Just as Michael registered a distant rumbling sound, a flash of light blinded him and he held up his arm to shield his face, the beam illuminating them like a spot-light. "Get back." He dragged Josie towards the trees as a truck came down the road. "What if it's him?"

"Different car." Josie pulled away and waved her arms over her head, making the pickup slow down, before finally coming to a stop in front of them.

"Lost. Err… Nostotros estamos perdidas." Josie's words echoed down the lonely road.

The man got out of the truck and walked over to them. His face looked tired, like someone after a long day at work, someone who could not be bothered with whatever drama they had to throw his way. The light from the car cast shadows over his face, accentuating the deep lines around his eyes. "Subir al camion."

"What did he say?" Michael asked Josie, but she looked as confused as him.

"Que?" she got closer.

"My English is not so good." He said looking bewildered as to what they were doing in the woods, in the dark.

Michael stood by as they tried to understand each other and spoke to each other in a jumble of Spanish and English.

"He says we can stay with him and his wife tonight, just down the road. He said we can eat. Sleep. I didn't want to complicate things by mentioning the police, or what happened. He seems nice. Legit." She spoke emphatically in her desperation to convince him.

"I don't know Josie."

"Well, what do you suggest? We're more in danger out here. Out in the open. At least if we go with him we can rest up. Sort this shit out in the morning. He's not going to wait forever."

"Fine." Michael felt like he could sleep forever. His heavy legs desperate to give way beneath him.

"Gracias, muchos gracias." Michael tried to express his gratitude, but came up short. He opened the heavy door to sit in the front passenger seat and Josie got in the back. The driver introduced himself as Antonio, and he and Josie talked while Michael spaced out and looked out the window. They had barely driven two minutes before Antonio's small house came into view. A little dog ran towards the truck, barking and bounding playfully. Antonio parked up and opened the driver's side door. "Abajo. Picco, no. Abajo," he said to the dog as it jumped up at his legs.

"Say hola to Picco." He picked up the dog under one arm. It had the glistening, bulging eyes of a chihuahua, but crossed with some other breed.

"Hola Picco." Josie leaned in and petted the dog on the head. "Buen chico." She had a big, goofy grin. Michael could barely believe she had let her guard down so quickly, as if they hadn't almost died earlier.

As they walked through the front door, they could hear the high-pitched wails of a baby crying, and the sounds of a mother desperately trying to soothe it. Picco jumped up and down, yapping. Steam emanated from the kitchen where the sound of a pot bubbling and savory smells filled the air. Rustic and full of life. Michael dodged some building blocks that littered the floor.

Antonio shouted into the kitchen. "Tenemos invitados."

A woman emerged. Her full cheeks bright red from the heat of the kitchen. She rested the child on her hip. "Hola." She looked bewildered, and Antonio filled her in. "No hablo Ingles Me llamo Gabriela." She spoke softly, and Michael could already feel his guard go down.

Josie introduced herself, and Michael nodded along like he knew what she was saying. Gabriela seemed to accept whatever Josie was saying graciously and got her to work setting the table.

"Can I do anything?" Michael asked.

"You could watch the baby while she finishes cooking."

"Um. I wouldn't know what to do with it." He tried to temper the look of terror that was inevitably in his eyes.

"Okay. You put these out. I'll look after the baby." She handed him a pile of plates.

Michael put the plates on the table and placed one at each seat whilst trying to remember which side of the plate the knife and fork went. People always laughed at him for putting them on the wrong side, even though he was right-handed. It occurred to him that none of this even mattered and couldn't help but laugh that he was worrying about something so insignificant. Gabriela emerged from the kitchen again, carrying two pots, and smiled at him as she put them in the center of the wooden table. There was something ceremonious about laying out the table. They'd even put out a tablecloth. This is just how Michael had imagined it—family.

They all sat down to a dinner of squash and beans in a rich brown sauce with warm tortillas. Despite how delicious it tasted and smelled, it was hard to get down. The left-over adrenaline wouldn't allow him to let his guard down. Eating wasn't allowed in fight-or-flight mode.

In-between bites, Josie babbled incoherent baby talk to the child next to her and smiled as the mother attempted to try to get at least some of the food in the baby's mouth, rather than everywhere else. Michael briefly wondered what lay in store for this child, what kind of suffering and trials waited in his future.

As he saw Josie smile, he knew she was meant for this world. She interacted with everyone around her, while he sat there, disconnected, a mere observer. He was glad the baby was there. It distracted everyone enough so Michael could keep to himself without having to pretend to fit in. Everyone lavished the baby with attention, revolving around it like it was the sun and they were powerless in its orbit.

Antonio and Gabriela shared their room with the baby and gave Josie and Michael a fleece blanket. The couch was theirs for the night. They started a small fire, especially for their last-minute guests, and Michael and Josie gazed at the fireplace as embers crackled and popped.

"See. I told you I had a good feeling about that guy. He said he'll drive us into town in the morning when he goes into work. Then we go straight to the police, in the light of day."

"Sounds good."

"You okay? You've been quiet all night." She shook her head as if realizing how ridiculous the words sounded. "About what happened earlier—"

"Maybe we should just go to sleep. I'm beat." Michael wasn't ready to tackle that particular minefield yet.

"How should we do this then?" Josie held the blanket in her arms.

"I could take the armchair, you can take the couch?"

"There's plenty of room on the couch for two, besides, there's only one blanket. Scooch." She gestured for him to make room.

"Just so you know, I like to be the little spoon." He joked.

"Noted." She laughed, and laid the blanket over him and got underneath, laying on her back, looking up at the ceiling. "Just so you know, I like being little spoon too. I can see this being a problem." She didn't say anything else, and turned onto her side, facing the living room with her back to him. He took that as an invitation and put his arm over her, wrapping it around her waist and holding her close to him. She let out a long sigh, as if her troubles were being expelled from her lungs and she held her arm over his and wiggled back a little so they were even closer. He took a deep breath, inhaling the smell of her hair. The scent of floral shampoo and coconut sunscreen reminded him of the resort where they met, before things had all got so complicated. He tilted his head forward towards her neck, wanting to disappear in the warmth before he had to face whatever fresh hell tomorrow would bring.

Chapter Eighteen

He went to shout but ended up sucking warm cloth into his mouth. His nostrils flared, but no oxygen was getting in. It was completely black as something covered his whole head and muffled screams came from his left. Even through the thick fabric of his head covering, he recognized Josie's cries and felt her next to him as someone forced him to his knees and bound his hands behind his back.

"Shut it, gringo."

Michael could just about make out the words, unable to recall the voice. It wasn't Julio.

"We're getting up now. Keep calm. If you don't struggle, I will leave this nice family alone with their brains intact. What do you say?"

Something cold and hard pressed against his temple; the steel muzzle of the gun dug through the fabric of the hood into the side of his head. A moment ago he had been enveloped in the blissful ignorance of sleep, and he couldn't force words out of his mouth.

"What do you say?" The stern voice repeated.

He nodded and groaned as he was dragged up to his feet. As they pulled him along, he could barely stay upright as his legs refused to cooperate. He only realized they were outside when the night air brushed his arms and as he took another step, there was nothing there, and he fell forward, smacking against the ground, chest first, with no arms to break the fall. The whole front of his body stung with the impact and he tried to suck in air again, in shock, as if he had been plunged into icy cold water. There was no strength left in him, and he let his captor drag him along, hoist him up, and slam him against something solid. Barely able to tell which way was which, Michael realized he was horizontal, his head and feet touching metal. A weight struck him at his side, another warm body writhed next to him. "Josie?" He shouted through his hood.

"It's me. I'm here."

A slam above them made it darker than it already was, as if that was even possible. He was certain he was in the trunk of a car, cramped, squished up against Josie, barely able to move. The feeling of suffocating made him feel like he in the deepest-darkest-depths of the ocean, with meters of water bearing down on top of him. The pressure was too much. To keep himself sane, he concentrated on the task at hand, and his fingers contorted, trying to get purchase on the rope around his wrists. He hooked one of his fingers in a gap in between the knot and yanked at it, trying to loosen it. Warm vibrations rolled through him as the engine started up and the car began to move. Josie rolled into him as the car jolted forward, and his finger slipped out of the knot he was working to undo. It was almost impossible to concentrate once the car traveled at full speed.

"Turn around." Josie's words were choked.

He didn't think and complied with her request. Her hand brushed his as she reached for the rope. It hadn't even occurred to him that they would be able to get a better angle if they worked on each other's ties. The brain was a mysterious organ when in panic mode. It didn't take her long to untie him, and he let out an elated cry when he could move his arms, and felt the blood rushing back to his numb hands. He ripped the hood off of his head, banging his arm on the side of the car in his rush, and pulled hers off. "It's okay. I've got this." He shimmied back around and got to work on her ropes. His fingers could barely feel them, and he fumbled wildly like a teenage boy trying to unclasp his girlfriend's bra. Why couldn't he do it? Why was he so useless? He became more frustrated, and then the car came to a stop. Fuck, he muttered under his breath, yanking at the ropes, probably making them even tighter somehow. Something finally gave, and he managed to pull the strings apart. She rolled over to face him and the car started again.

"I'm sorry. I'm so sorry." A tear on her cheek glistened in the darkness.

"Shh. It's fine." He didn't believe that in the slightest.

"We're going to die. You're going to die because of me," she sniffed.

"Hey, don't talk like that, not yet." He took her head between his hands. "It's not over until it's over." He wondered where he had pulled that platitude from.

"It's over."

"I'm sure I read somewhere once. If you get locked in the trunk of a car, you should kick the headlights out, and then you can stick your hand out through the gap and wave for help."

For some unknown reason, she snorted with laughter. "Where the hell did you read that?"

"Damned if I know. Who knew that snippet would come in handy?" It was comforting to know that all the time he had wasted watching TV wasn't all for nothing.

"Don't you think that's just the kind of thing that would piss him off even more?"

"I think whoever it is, is already as pissed off they're gonna get. This is our only chance."

"Will it even work?" He heard her lightly kick her foot against the end of the trunk. "Shit. We're stopping again." She went still, and they lay there, listening. The lid of the trunk flew open and two figures loomed above, the sky behind them tinged purple with the oncoming sunrise.

"Well, I can see you managed to free yourselves. Bravo." The man clapped. Michael had never been unnerved by someone clapping before. The sound of his hands slapping together rang out in the still morning, and it didn't stop, but Michael wondered what would happen when it did.

"Samuel!" Julio shouted and chucked the man a shovel he had grabbed from the car.

The man Julio referred to as Samuel, caught the shovel in midair and held it in both hands as Julio slammed the car door shut.

"Get out." Samuel demanded. Josie lifted herself out of the trunk and Samuel pulled her clear of the car, checking her over. "And you." He rested the shovel at his feet and pointed his gun at Michael. "We don't have all day. Vamanos."

It felt like a dream, like he was paralyzed and no amount of will could force his legs to move.

"I'm not going to ask again." He turned the gun on Josie, pulling her towards him as he pressed the gun to her chest.

"Okay. Okay." He scrambled up onto his hands and knees and jumped out. It would appear with the right motivation, anything was possible.

"Bravo. So you're not completely useless. How does it feel to know your girl has more balls than you?"

"She's not—"

"Did I ask you to speak?" Samuel spat. He had asked Michael a question, so in a sense he had asked him to speak, but he thought it best not to point that out. This man that stood before him was a good few inches taller than Michael. He wore a dark shirt, his mustache and beard were perfectly manicured and his thick hair slicked back. "Grab the shovel."

Michael looked down at the shovel on the floor. It would make a good weapon, except Samuel clearly had another purpose for it.

"Am I speaking English? Pick up the shovel already."

The shovel was heavier than he thought it would be and he hauled it up, considering how much force it would take to cave in this guy's skull with it, or if he was even capable of such a thing. All eyes were on him, including a third man he hadn't noticed who got out of the driver's seat. If he even tried it, he had no doubt he would be riddled with bullet holes before he could even get the first hit in.

"Rapido. Get digging." Samuel pointed to a spot on the floor. "What are you waiting for?"

Chapter Nineteen

The land in front of them was an empty wasteland in the oasis that surrounded it. This was where dreams went to die. Except for the odd bit of garbage, and a shrub here and there, there was nothing. He had imagined dying in his hotel room, air-con on, some relaxing music in the background, all the drinks he could fit inside him, and a comfortable bed to lie on, not this. Digging his own grave in the middle of what looked like an enormous abandoned building site was not what he'd had in mind. He prayed that at least they would shoot him first. Being buried alive was the worst thing he could imagine, that and drowning. A gunshot to the head. It would be messy, but it would be fast. A micro-second of pain, for an eternity of ignorant bliss, sent back to the void from which he came. He couldn't remember anything before he was born, or anything when he was asleep, besides his dreams, and he assumed it would be like that. He'd come to terms with his own death a long time ago, but the thought of Josie, buried in a shallow grave here, it wasn't right.

"Stop," Samuel barked his order, and everyone listened.

The five of them stood in the middle of nowhere. Michael waited for them to make their move.

"Dig." Samuel half-heartedly waved his gun at them and then stashed it back in the holster, as if he was certain they would do what he said. Julio still held his gun out, keeping his arms raised in front of him. His arms shook, lacking Samuel's confidence. The third man passed Josie a shovel, and then stood still as a statue, saying nothing.

"Dig."

"Why would I dig my own grave?" Josie yelled defiantly.

Samuel's mouth hung open in shock that she dare even ask such a question, then his open mouth turned to a strange grin as he shook his head and tutted. "Ah, sweet girl." He stepped up to her and bent his knees, bringing his face level with hers. "There are so many things worse than death, and you don't want to know what they are. Play nice, and maybe you'll never have to find out." He brought his face even closer, so they were almost touching. "Now dig."

She glared at him as she struck the earth below with the head of her shovel. The look on her face resembled a teenager sulking at having to tidy their room, or something equally mundane.

"See, that wasn't so hard, was it?" He turned to Michael. "What are you staring at? Get digging."

Michael made his first attempt and weakly thrust at the earth with his shovel. It was softer than it had looked, but still hard going. He had to drag this out as long as possible.

"Ha ha, she can dig better than you too." Samuel lit a cigarette and watched them with a smirk on his face. "Ah, Julio. What would you do without me? You were never very good at following through." He paced up and down, taking small, sharp drags of his cigarette and kicking up dirt with his shoe. "Put some backbone into it guys."

Michael decided it was time. If they were going to die anyway, they might as well make a bid for freedom. He and Josie had their shovels. Samuel's gun wasn't in his hand. If Josie took out Julio and he took out Samuel at the same time, then all that would be left, would be one man. He glanced over him to see if he was armed but couldn't tell. He wondered why this man was here, anyway. He did nothing, just watched. Josie looked down at what she was doing, and he tried to catch her eye. They needed to be on the same page.

It was almost fully light now, and the residual orange hue of sunrise was fading fast. Michel scooped another shovel-full of earth and threw it to the side in a pile. He had seen someone dig their own grave in a film once and found himself wondering how someone could do something so stupid. Now he understood. The body seeks to delay pain as long as possible. And he could only imagine how someone who didn't want to die would react in the situation he was in. No matter how much he wanted to go, it wasn't time, not yet.

"What did you do with my sister? If you're going to kill me, at least give me that. Please." She moved towards Samuel, and Michael tensed immediately. Don't to it, he repeated over and over in his head as he watched Samuel's relaxed stance turn defensive.

He took a drag on his cigarette as he locked eyes with her and blew a stream of smoke in her face. "Nah. Keep digging. Once this is done, maybe then I will tell you."

She threw the shovel to the ground and fell to her knees. Silent tears streamed down her face and the sobs only came when she put her head in-between her knees. Michael went to comfort her. "I don't think so." Samuel stepped across Josie and planted his hand on Michael's shoulder. "Keep digging."

A shot rang out, filling the empty space like the shockwaves of a nuclear blast. Before Michael knew what the hell was going on Julio dropped to the floor, blood gushing from the side of his head.

Chapter Twenty

Samuel must have been as surprised as Michael had, as it took him a moment before he reached for his gun. As Samuel aimed at the other man, Michael swung the shovel at his head with a force he didn't even know he was capable of. Samuel's shot went off in the wrong direction as he crashed down to the floor and ricocheted off the car.

Michael stood there as Josie curled in a ball in front of him. The man still had his gun raised, and Michael wondered if he was next, yet still couldn't bring himself to move.

"Vamanos." The man shouted, "Get in the car."

Josie took her hands from the side of her head and looked up at the man.

"The car, now!" Don't make me regret this."

Michael helped Josie up from the floor and they walked shakily towards the car, trying not to look in the direction of Julio's lifeless corpse. When they were both in the backseat, Michael pressed against the dusty window to see the man stride over to Samuel. He towered over him. Michael half expected him to shoot him in the head, but all he did was nudge him in the side with his foot, checking for signs of life. Samuel's cell-phone slipped from his pocket onto the ground, and the man smashed it under his shoe before heading back to the car.

The man got in the driver's seat, started the engine and turned around, heading back in the direction they had come from. Josie looked out the back window as the car picked up speed. "You're just going to leave him there. Is he dead?"

"I'll never kill a man if I don't have to. Besides, if I killed Samuel Hernandez, I would be as good as dead, no matter where I went. At least if I leave him alive, they probably won't bother to come looking."

"What about Julio?" She asked, still looking out the back window.

"No-one gives a shit about Julio. Glorified mule."

"Who was that guy? Samuel. I don't understand," she stuttered.

"Samuel Valentino Hernandez is someone you want nothing to do with. You need to go home. You need to be on a plane. Go home."

"You mean that wasn't nasty?" The pounding in Michael's chest would not subside, and he looked out the back window again, half-expecting Samuel to be following behind them. Indestructible, like the villain of some horror franchise.

"Let me put it this way. I will be getting my family the fuck out of here before he even has a chance to wake up and get back to the main road."

"Family?" Michael asked, somehow surprised that man who just shot someone in cold blood would have people he loved waiting for him at home. Hell, it was more than he had.

"We're getting the fuck out. I'm just a driver. I was not meant for this shit."

"Where are you going?" Josie asked.

"I think that's enough questions, don't you?" He checked his rear view mirror.

"I'm not finished." Josie pushed her luck. "My sister. Do you know if they had her? What did they want with her?"

"Ismael Garcia." He spoke the words as if they should mean something.

"What? Who is Ismael Garcia?" Josie took a slow, measured breath, trying to keep her cool.

"We used to share a car. We couldn't even afford a heap of junk car, so we brought one together. I'd do day shift, he'd do night shift. Eventually we had enough to upscale, started our own little company." His tone was surprisingly matter of fact, given what he was telling her.

"Ismael?" She mouthed, committing the name to memory. "Did he? Did you?" Her voice caught in her throat.

"Ismael borrowed money from Samuel. I never would have started the company with him if I knew how he got it. Once you owe them you're fucked. I just wanted to be a taxi driver. Take tourist around. It wasn't the best money, but it was an honest living. I'm a simple man. I see where greed gets you."

"Who took her? Tell me straight. Tell me now." She demanded in a hoarse scream.

"Ismael did it as a favor to Samuel."

"What the hell did Samuel want. Money? He got the money. Pretty much everything our parent's had. Why didn't he let her go?"

"Samuel was just the middle-man. Arranged it for his boss. She must have put up a fight, got herself killed." He met her eyes in the rear-view mirror, a flicker of sympathy hid behind his matter-of-fact voice.

"Oh god," she wailed, burying her head into the seat in front, covering her face with her hands. Michael went to reach out, but something stopped him. He gave her space to process what she was told.

"I'm sorry," Miguel said weakly.

"So who's his boss? They won't get away with it. I won't let them." She was upright again, and in detective mode after wiping tears from her face.

"I never met the man, but trust me, he's a guy you do not want to be messing with."

"You expect me to believe that?" Her voice elevated to a scream.

"Believe what you want. It's the truth," he said calmly, seemingly unfazed.

"Okay. What about Julio? What does he have to do with all of this?"

"Julio's a nobody. He helps get dope across the border from Belize. Only small amounts, nothing earth shattering. He does a run every once and a while, they leave his hotel alone. That's the deal."

"Samuel's boss, do you know his name?"

"His real name, no. Everyone calls him El Verdugo."

Michael had been so engrossed, listening to what they were saying, that he only noticed the light hissing noise as the car slowed to a stop.

"What happened?" Josie's head turned from side to side fast enough to give anyone whiplash.

"I don't know?" The man got out and inspected the front of the car. "Mierda."

Not that he knew much about cars, but Michael got out to see what was going on. The man knelt down and ran his finger over a hole in the front of the car. As he got up and opened the front bonnet, steam poured out. "Mierda." He slammed the bonnet shut and slammed his clenched fist against the metal.

"What it is?" Michael asked, pretty sure he already knew the answer.

"El radiador." He kicked the bottom of the car and zig-zagged in the middle of the road, muttering obscenities.

"This can't be happening." Josie leaned against the car in defeat. "What do we do now?"

Josie pulled her cell-phone from her pocket and pushed the on button, but it was dead. "Do you have someone you can call? Sorry in all the chaos, I never got your name." She trailed behind him.

"I'm Miguel. There is a rest-stop, maybe three miles away, it will be quicker to walk."

"You have the same name."

"What?" he muttered, glancing back at her for a second. The ridiculousness of the statement made them wonder if Josie was in shock.

"Miguel is Spanish for Michael, right?"

Michael wondered how he could have gone his whole life without knowing that, when he heard a rumble coming. "Is that?"

Squinting as he stared into the distance, one of Miguel's hands hovered over his weapon. "Not them," he said as the car cruised closer. "Samuel has no way of contacting anyone anyway, we should have bought ourselves some time."

Josie looked concerned. "Shall we flag them down?" The car was in danger of driving right past them until Miguel made the call, and started waving his arms. Much to Michael's surprise the dark red Nissan pulled over to the side of the road. Pulsating bass sent vibrations they could feel through the ground until the driver turned the music down. The front car window slid down and Miguel talked to the driver so quickly Michael couldn't even pick out a single word he was saying. He could just make out the driver as he peered through the crack in the open window. A young curly-haired man, with a nonchalant look, and one of the most garish shirts Michael had ever seen. "No hay problema." The man smiled.

Chapter Twenty One

In the car, Josie's knees were almost up to her chin as she propped her feet up on a bag lodged in the foot-well, and a guitar propped up in-between her and Michael. Leaning forward, she gave him a serious look. "When we get to town. I will book you the next flight out of here, on me. I had no idea things would get this out of hand."

"I'm going back to the hotel where we met. I have things to do."

"What could be important enough to risk your life for?" she asked with an annoyed frown on her face.

"It's complicated. You're going home though, right?" If he could just get her on a flight out of there, he could finish his business without worrying about her.

"I have things to do too." She crossed her arms and turned away.

"Are you serious?" He hadn't realized how loud his voice had gotten, and the driver shot him a glance through the rear-view mirror. He lowered his voice. "You're not going to do any good if you're dead. Do you want your parents to mourn two daughters, what good would that do?"

"But they're not mourning Michael, they're in limbo. They keep thinking one day she's just going to walk in the front door with some crazy story, like oh hey mom, hey dad, so I ended up working at this yoga retreat, and yeah, sorry I forgot to call you for a year. Oh right, the kidnapping. Yeah, I got away, sorry, did I forget to tell you that?"

"Well, I think it's time that everybody faced facts. People die. Life is cruel and random. Justice is some made up concept to make people feel better about the fact that the world is just one big chaotic mess. It means nothing."

"Fuck you, Michael. You don't know what it's like."

"Okay, I'm sorry. That was insensitive. I—"

"Can you just stop talking, please." She turned her back to him and stared out of the window.

His chest tightened as he realized he had just alienated the one person who he gave a shit about. Why couldn't he just contain his outburst? It wasn't Josie's fault that life had dealt him a deck of crap. It was the unfairness of it all he couldn't stand. How someone as useless as him, someone who didn't even want to live, would still be here, yet Josie's sister wasn't.

How his mother could die randomly, yet his neglectful piece-of-shit dad was alive and well.

"Hear me out." He reached out to her. "I will do whatever it takes to help you find out what happened. Even if I have to march up to El Verdugo myself. Trust me, I have absolutely nothing to lose, except for you."

She turned her head to face him, her expression softening. "I'm all you have to lose? Wow. I feel kinda bad for you right now. I mean, that is sad."

"I'm tragic. What else can I say?" He shrugged.

"Seriously though, I've been so caught up in all of my baggage. I'm sorry. I feel like you have a story to tell. Why are you here? What's your deal, Michael?"

"To be honest, I don't really want to talk about it."

"Oh my god, that's such a cop out. Come on. Tell me one thing about yourself that no-one else knows."

"Trust me, there's nothing to know. My life is as dull as they come." He averted his gaze to the seat in front of him.

"I don't believe that," she pushed.

"Okay, fine. One fact about me. I was homeless once."

"Woah crap. That's heavy. What happened?" She leaned in even closer.

"I don't really want to go into it."

"You can't drop a bomb like that on me and then not tell me how it happened." She looked at him expectantly, but he didn't speak. "Fine. I get it. You're the strong and silent type."

"I'm the silent and silent type." He joked, glad she had dropped it.

"On a serious note though, the guy Miguel mentioned. Samuel's boss. El Verdugo. You know what the name El Verdugo means, right?" Her face turned deadly serious.

"No, what?" he asked, slumped in his chair.

"It means, The Executioner."

Michael sat upright. "Oh, shit."

Chapter Twenty Two

The driver left them on a random street in Chetumal, as Miguel did not want them to know where he lived. "This way." Miguel announced. His plan was to get his wife, child, and anything that they could fit into their arms and to get far, far away. Miguel had people he could reach out to. He agreed to them coming to his house so that they could take some fresh clothes and a charger for Josie's phone. Beyond that, they had no plan.

As they continued walking, the houses went from one story, to two stories, with balconies overlooking a church. There were still little reminders of where they were. Spikes on the top of the walls to stop people climbing up, and bars in front of the windows, but they were ornate enough to distract you from their purpose. A group of locals congregated at the end of the street, and Michael stopped Josie in her tracks. Miguel burst into a sprint, running towards the crowd, and Josie went to follow him.

"Careful." Michael warned. There was something about the look on the people's faces that made him go cold. Open-mouthed, eyes wide, and holding their hands up to their faces, in the blur of chaos they resembled The Scream. Whatever they had seen had rendered them into the horror of that painting. When Miguel got to the end of the road, he fell to his knees, and the sound that came out of his mouth, was one Michael recognized, a sound he knew too well, when there was nothing left, and you couldn't control the noises that came out of you, when every last modicum of inhibition had evaporated, and pain was the only thing left.

They inched towards the scene until they could see what everyone was looking at. The body hung from the balcony, dangling limply like a puppet, slit down the middle and entrails hanging down from the cavity, blood dripping onto the floor below. Her skin looked grey.

"Oh god." Josie gasped, clamping her hand over her mouth.

Michael wanted to run to Miguel, but his legs were planted to the spot. The image tore him in two. He couldn't comprehend what was happening in Miguel's mind right at that moment. Josie ducked behind a garbage can and her body convulsed as she vomited. He didn't want to, but for some reason he looked back at what he believed to be

Miguel's wife. More people had gathered, like rubberneckers at the site of a car crash. Miguel's cries of grief still filled the air. He had to help, not that he could, but he felt the need to be at his side. As Michael got closer men in black uniform infiltrated the crowd, they looked like police officers. Hopefully now they would take this seriously. One of the men grabbed Miguel's arms and cuffed them behind his back.

"No. What are you doing?" Michael shouted, but his voice was lost in the noise of the crowd.

Miguel tried to wrestle his way free, thrashing around like an animal upon hearing the door of a trap shut behind them. The harder he struggled, the more officers came to restrain him, pinning him roughly against the floor, his cheek pressed against the concrete. It was obvious—the moment he gave up—his body, lifeless on the floor. The men in black hoisted him up, dragging him towards the police car.

"We need to get out of here." Michael tried to get her to move, but she lowered herself down against the wall, snatching in quick shallow breaths. "Come on. We know who did this, and we're next." He stood above her offering a hand, but she started shaking on the floor. Lowing himself down to her level, he took her tear soaked cheeks in his hands. "Just breathe okay. Nice and slow." He inched back to give her some space. If years of experience had taught him anything, it taught him that you couldn't fight your way through a panic attack with sheer force. He peered around the corner of the wall that shielded them. The body had already been cut down, and the house swarmed with police. As he turned back, her breathing had already calmed somewhat. Michael wiped tears away from his face that he hadn't even realized were there. "Are you okay to move now? We can find somewhere safer, and then you can take all the time you need." She nodded, and Michael pulled her up with both hands.

"I can't walk anymore." Josie sat on a wall, shoulders slumped and her arms hanging down limply in front of her.

"We can take a break." Michael looked around for anywhere suitable to lay-low for a few minutes but came up blank. They had no money. No belongings. Nothing. He put his hands in his empty pockets and the anxiety rose in him like bile.

"We're fucked Michael."

The panic in her voice made him feel even worse. Even though the air was warm, he shivered, and the streets looked cold and grey. Any last bit of charm had long since vanished. "Maybe we go to the police." He had no idea what else to suggest at this point.

Josie snorted. "I can't even imagine where I would begin explaining this. Why did they arrest Miguel, I wonder? Do they know about Julio?"

"Maybe, although I don't think it's in Samuel's interest for them to look too far into all that." He tried his best to sound convincing.

"I don't trust the police. We need to go to the British consulate. I think that's our safest bet. We need someone on our side. The way they arrested Miguel was just…"

"Where is the consulate?" It was time to get practical, not to waste time speculating.

"The consulate is in Cancún. The embassy is in Mexico city."

"What's the difference?" he asked, wondering if he had just asked one of those questions that should have been obvious.

Josie seemed to be in her own world now, staring off into the distance. "I don't even have change for a pay-phone. You ever begged for money before?" She rifled through her pockets but came up empty.

"I have an idea." Michael started walking in the direction of the waterfront.

Chapter Twenty Three

If there was going to be a hotel or hostel anywhere, it was going to be by the sea. His eyes scanned the line of shops along the waterfront, starting to recognize the scenery from where Julio had taken them to go on his yacht. A fantasy popped into his head of riding Julio's boat off into the sunset with Josie and living off the land on an island in Belize. He could learn to fish.

There was something comforting about walking alongside the bars and restaurants. No matter where you were in the world, beer always brought people together. Watching others sat outside with cold drinks, relaxing, laughing, and joking began to make Michael envious. That could have been him working his way through the cocktail list back in Tulum. Their beaming smiles made him angry. Why did some people find it so easy to be happy?

"What about there?" Josie stopped and pointed towards a building a few yards ahead of them.

"Perfect." Michael burst into a jog towards the hostel and slowed down as they reached the entrance. They walked in through the two open doors, a group of travelers huddled in a nook in the corner, all talking over each other with excitable energy.

"Can I help?" The lady behind the counter asked. Her black hair slicked back in a ponytail tight enough to give her a facelift, giving her a severe look.

Josie burst into tears at the front desk and the receptionist's face changed as she realized what a state they were in.

"Oh no, what is wrong." She walked around the desk and put an arm around Josie's shoulder.

"We were mugged. They had a knife." Josie buried her face in her hands. "They took all our money. We didn't know where to go. I need to charge my phone."

"Of course. Poor thing." She disappeared behind the desk and grabbed a white plastic box full of chargers, adapters, and other electronics that looked like they had been left behind by guests.

"There are plug sockets around the corner where those people are." She pointed. "The police station is not far, but by all means charge your phone here. You need anything else?"

"Water? If that's okay?"

"Of course. Uno momento." She hurried out back to fetch them a cup of water.

"Michael." A hand clamped down on his shoulder, making his heart leap in his chest. "Is that you?" It took Michael's brain a good few seconds to process who stood before him.

"Aleksander. Fuck. It's so good to see you." Something about the harrowing events of the day, and seeing a familiar face hit him like a swift kick to the gut and he hugged Aleksander, squeezing him tight.

"Woah. At least buy me a drink first." He laughed and looked Michael over. "You okay? You look like shit."

"You don't know the half of it. This is such a coincidence. I can't believe it." He looked Alex up and down again, as if he were a mirage that would disappear into nothing in front of his eyes.

"Trust me, not a coincidence. I keep bumping into people I have met along the way. The gringo trail y'know. I've seen this girl I met in Mexico City three times now. She just keeps popping up y'know."

"Is Anna and Freja here?" Michael asked.

"No. They are living in Chiapas." He glanced over at Josie. "So… who is your friend?"

"Sorry, so rude of me. This is Josie. We met in Tulum." He hoped Josie could keep it together.

"Hello Josie." He shook her hand. "What's wrong." He said as he noticed her red, puffy face.

"Oh, it's just—"

The member of staff emerged with two plastic cups of water and handed one to each of them. "These poor things got mugged." Michael didn't realize just how thirsty he was until he felt the water slide down his throat and let out an involuntary moan of pleasure.

"Oh, that must have been scary. Do you need anything? I can sort you out."

"Well we lost our wallets. Maybe I could transfer money to your account, then you could get it from an ATM for us?" Josie suggested. "We were just about to charge our phones."

"Why don't, we sit, I get you a nice cold beer while we sort this." It gave Michael whiplash to go from the horrors he had witnessed earlier, to being treated with kid-gloves. The fact that these almost perfect strangers seemed to care so much about his welfare felt strange and foreign to him.

By the time Josie had connected her phone, Aleksander had three bottles of beer, holding them with the necks in-between his fingers. "Ladies first." He passed one to Josie, one to Michael, and then opened his by cracking the cap against the edge of the table.

"You guys look like you're in shock no? Did they have a weapon?"

"What?" Josie jolted upright.

"The mugger."

Michael leaned towards Josie, his mouth near her ear. "Maybe we should tell him, maybe he can help."

Josie shot him a look that said, hell no. "I'm not getting anyone else involved in this. Miguel's wife. That's on me."

"How the hell is that on you? You didn't—"

"Guys. Guys. What's going on?" Although Aleksander looked concerned, there was a flash of curiosity behind his eyes.

"Do you have the Wi-Fi password?" Josie had the desperate look of a crack addict trying to get their fix.

"MANATEE123. All caps." Aleksander offered as three people burst into the front of the hostel erratically, talking over each other and flapping around like headless chickens.

"Did you hear?" Everyone piped down for the woman that spoke the loudest. "Someone was murdered. Apparently it happened about an hour ago. They said she was gutted and hung off of her balcony." There was something about her face, like she was excited somehow, that this was a thrilling story that she could tell all her friend's back home.

"Oh no." The receptionist's face dropped. "Gang related, I assume?"

"Not this time. The person I spoke to said they got a tip that the husband did it. They were having an argument or something, and the guy just lost it. Apparently they got the call as it was happening, but by the time police got there it was too late." From the tone of her voice, the casual passerby would probably assume she was just talking about a juicy piece of gossip or the latest celebrity indiscretion. Michael wondered if he was being unfair. This lady reminded him of an irritating person he used to work with, who would always try to get everyone involved in the office politics, feeding off of others' conflict. He looked over at Josie to see how she was taking this, and she unplugged her phone and ran out the front doors.

"Hang on." He leaned on the central table as he got up and ran after her to find her pacing in front of the building whilst looking at her phone. "Don't worry. We can clear Miguel. We just need to say he was with us when it happened. They'll find out the truth Josie. It will be fine."

"What about this is fine exactly." She thrust her phone screen at his face and Michael took it from her hands and zoomed in on the picture.

"What the fuck?" He squinted at the image, hoping it would somehow change before his eyes. He was seeing things. He was sleep deprived. His own face looked back up at him, a photograph of Josie next to him.

Wanted in connection with the disappearance of Julio Vasquez.

A rush of blood ran into his face as the sun burned down on him. The most trouble he had gotten into with the law, was the one time he tried shoplifting as a teenager. He felt exposed, like everyone passing on the street would recognize him at any second. "Is this some sort of joke?"

"If it is, I'm not fucking laughing." She continued pacing and his eyes followed her, her pacing made him even more anxious.

"We really need to get to the embassy. Sort all this out. They'll see through it. What were they thinking, though? Surely it's not in Samuel's interest to have them look into all this. But he's forcing our hand. Giving us no choice but end up in jail."

"Is he just trying to keep us busy? I don't know." She flung her hands up in the air, as if she was praying for the answers to come dropping down from the sky.

A figure appeared in Michael's peripheral vision and he turned to see Aleksander stood in the doorway. "I know something is wrong, I'm not stupid. Please, let me help."

"We need somewhere to stay. Somewhere private. Alex, someone's after us." Michael couldn't keep it in any longer. They couldn't do this by themselves.

"I'm moving into my long-term rental place tomorrow. I was supposed to move in today, but I was thinking to try my luck with this girl here. I was getting all the signals, you know. I was thinking of being a scuba instructor, thought I'd get a nice little place to stay, comes with a car too. You can stay as long as you want."

"Why would you do that for me? You barely even know me?" The promise of somewhere safe to catch his breath was more than he could have hoped for.

"We travelers need to stick together, y'know."

"Alex, there are things you don't know. Things that if you knew, you would not want us staying with you."

"Then you tell me tonight, I can at least give you a good night's sleep." He walked up to the front desk. "Anita. Hola. I check out today after all. If Katie ask after me, do you think you could give her my number?"

"Sure Alex. This place won't be the same without you. Hope the diving goes well." She gave him a brief hug over the counter before serving a new guest that was waiting.

Michael leaned against the window of the taxi, pretending to be asleep as Aleksander sat in front, chatting with the driver like they were two old friends catching up. He was an easy guy to like and could talk to anyone. It was a talent Michael wished he could possess, but he struggled to relate to people he had little in common with. Usually he didn't trust overly happy people. He felt they were lying to themselves, phony, projecting a fake version of themselves to get people to like them, yet he found Aleksander's childlike optimism inexplicably endearing. Josie also kept her head down in the back of the cab. Nothing to see here, just two weary travelers, exhausted from all the overnight buses, activities and nights of endless drinking.

The taxi pulled in front of a white rectangular building with a mural of waves painted on the side in bold-blue. The entire process of checking in was discreet, involving no human interaction whatsoever. Aleksander put a code into the keypad of a lockbox to retrieve the front door and garage key, and a card with the Wi-Fi code sat in there with a handwritten note.

"Welcome to casa Janssen." Alex announced as he struggled to get the knack of the stiff lock.

The guest suite was minimalist and clean. The main living space had a large, almost brand new sofa bed and an adjoining kitchen. The bedroom had just enough room for the king-size bed, but little else, and there was a small bathroom between them.

"So I guess you guys better fill me in." Alex sat at the end of the sofa and cracked open a beer he got from his bag. Josie excused herself and went to the bathroom.

"I honestly don't know where to begin. I met Josie in Tulum, at the hotel bar. We hit it off. It turned out she came to Mexico to find her sister. She got kidnapped a year ago, around here actually."

"Oh my god. Are you for serious?"

"Unfortunately, yes. Anyway, I agreed to help her. She wanted to find out what happened. Go rogue, and somehow find out something the police couldn't, or just didn't want to find. I honestly didn't think anything would come of it. We asked around. Got ourselves noticed. Alex, someone tried to kill us."

"That's insane. So what did you do?"

"That's just it. There's nothing we can do. Something bigger than us is going on here. That woman that got killed, she was not murdered by her husband like the girl at the hostel said. He was with us. He saved us. Now he's been arrested, and they're after us now. They're looking for us, the cops are, and this other guy, Samuel Valentino Hernandez. He wants us gone. He has something to do with her sister going missing, I don't know if he is cartel, or what." Michael snatched in a breath.

"Slow down. This is a lot to take in. Jesus." He got up from the sofa and started pacing whilst taking sips of his beer.

"You've got to help us. We need to get to the embassy, tell them our side of the story before any police involvement. All we need is the money to get there and we can be out of your hair."

"I can drive you. It's probably safer that way."

"That is more than we would have ever asked for. Are you sure?" He tried to keep eye contact with Alex as he paced the room. He needed to know he was serious.

"Of course." Alex sat back on the sofa.

"We don't want you to get in trouble for our sake though. Josie already blames himself for Miguel's wife."

"Is that the one that died today?"

"Yeah." Michael sighed and ran his hand through his hair, it was getting in desperate need of a good trim. "There is one other thing you could do for me. I can pay you… although… if the police are looking for us, will they be keeping an eye on our bank accounts, I wonder?"

"Don't you worry. You pay me back when you can for anything. What is it you need, anyway?"

"Well, it's kind of two things, really. I left something important in a locker in a hotel in Arenales. It's probably not there still, but it's important, and I can't get anywhere near the place. They know me there." Michael's mouth seemed to work independently from his brain. He couldn't believe what he was asking.

"So you want me to pick up something for you?"

"If that's okay. Just quick, in and out. Book a night, check the locker. I hid it right at the back, so I'm hoping they didn't find it yet. I'll give you whatever money is left in my bank account."

"What is it?"

"I'd rather not say, but I wouldn't ask if it wasn't important."

"It's kind of exciting. Aleksander undercover. What's travel if not to have some crazy story to tell after, huh?"

Michael's conscience twinged like a faulty muscle. He assured himself that Aleksander was in no danger. They had no idea who he was, to them he was just some other traveler. The thing that really bothered him was what he was asking him to pick up. If he knew what he had been tasked with, would he even have agreed? Aleksander couldn't get into trouble; Pentobarbital was legal here. Michael knew Aleksander's curiosity would get the better of him, and he would have a look at what was inside the brown bag. Michael decided he would worry about it later and pushed the thoughts away.

"So what's the other thing?" Alex asked.

"Do you know if there is a drug-store near here?"

"What for?"

"I'll write you a list." Michael grabbed a pad of paper that had been kindly left by the owner by the phone and started scribbling down a grocery list.

Chapter Twenty Four

"I can't believe I'm doing this." Josie held the scissors against her long, sleek hair.

"It's just hair. It'll grow back. Do you want me to do it for you?"

"No, it's fine. I'll do it. Then I'll do yours. You know you look like you're wearing a mop on your head." It was the first hint of a smile, or an expression other than sadness or fear that he had seen on her face for a while.

The contents of a pack of hair box-dye was laid out on the kitchen counter: a sachet, two bottles, a pair of gloves, and an instruction manual. "What do I do with this?"

"Are you kidding, Michael? It's easy. Just read the directions. What is it with men not wanting to read instructions? It's like a sickness."

"But they're in Spanish."

"Look at the back. I'm sure it will have English on there."

Michael held the crinkled fold-out leaflet in front of his face, squinting at the small writing like he was a lost tourist reading a map.

Josie sighed. "Just mix the three bottles together, give it a shake, and slap it on. It's not rocket science. Give it here." She put the scissors down, took the biggest bottle and unscrewed it, adding the color sachet and the small bottle of oil to the developer before screwing the lid back on and giving it a vigorous shake. As she twisted the protective seal off of the main bottle, liquid erupted out the top like a volcano. "Here you go, try to get it even okay? Don't want you standing out more than you do already."

He squeezed a load of the creamy liquid on top of his head and rubbed it in with his bare hands.

"Michael, seriously? It's black hair dye, you're going to stain your hands. Careful not to get any on the floor either, because that will stain too."

He burst into uncontrollable hysterical laughter that shook his entire body and left him gasping for breath. One minute they were minutes from certain death, and the next they were worrying about getting a stain on the floor. Such things seemed so utterly insignificant now. He could see the ends of Josie's lips reluctantly turn up, as if she was desperately trying to keep her feelings bottled up, until the pressure was so much that it spewed out like that bottle of chemicals he was putting on his head. The great-heaving laughs wrenched their whole bodies until tears streamed down their faces, and they weren't sure if they were laughing or crying.

"What is going on in here?" Aleksander came from outside, bringing the smell of cigarettes in with him, and looked at them as if they had lost their minds. "Careful with that. I want to make sure I don't get charged for damage." His words only served to make them laugh harder, and his look of bemusement turned to laughter.

"Don't you think Michael will look really hot with black hair?" Josie said in-between gasps.

"Like a sexy Lego man." Aleksander laughed as he grabbed his fourth beer.

"Maybe we need a fake mustache to complete the disguise?" Josie added, red in the face.

"No, a sombrero. Maybe a poncho." Alex's released a series of short, high-pitched laughs.

"A newspaper with two eyeholes cut in it." Josie wiped tears from her eyes and let out a snort.

"Too far. Too much." Alex had started to calm down now and was capable of taking a sip of beer without the threat of having to spit it out with laughter.

"Alright, alright, relax. I'm not unleashing my new look just for fun. Besides, Josie is bleaching her hair next, so that's going to be something. Then all we need is a pair of shades and then poof, it's like we never existed."

"Shit." Josie snapped back to the reality of the situation. "I haven't even let my parents know I'm okay. There is no way I'm calling them. I'm just going to send a message."

"You should use a VPN so they can't track our IP address." Aleksander suggested, as if he only just realized the implication of harboring two potential fugitives. "So Michael. Tomorrow I go to the hotel?"

"Yeah. I don't think you should be driving tonight." Michael looked over at the row of bottles on the window-sill.

Chapter Twenty Five

Michael sat in the back seat with Josie, wondering how Aleksander managed to talk them into joining him, although, as he thought about it, he realized they were probably safer in Arelanes than they were in Chetumal. Hopefully, their change of appearance would be enough for them to stay in the back of the car unnoticed while Aleksander did his thing.

Michael glanced over at Josie. The harsh bleach had taken away some of the straightness, and her hair now fell in beachy waves. She looked like she'd fit in perfectly with Aleksander's diving buddies. The thought crossed his mind that they may not return from Arelanes today, or that they'd finish the day locked in some jail cell. As they reached the outskirts of town, Michael's hands grew clammy as he tried to keep his breathing and heart rate in check. He closed his eyes as he took in deep, controlled breaths. In. And out. In. And out. All he had to do was sit in the back of the car while Alex went to the hotel, but he felt sick, and his stomach groaned. The bumpy road didn't help. Looking for ways to distract himself, he decided to brief Alex. "Okay. So, why are you here?"

Aleksander turned the steering wheel, getting closer to the hotel. "I'm just stopping by. I came from Cancún, wanted somewhere to overnight before I go to Oaxaca."

"Good. Good. And why wouldn't you stay somewhere with more going on, like Chiapas."

"I've already been there. I want to get off the beaten track." Alex popped a piece of gum in his mouth and looked in the mirror, making sure his fringe was in check.

"Good." Michael's heart rate steadied. "And you remember what our bags look like? And what locker my package is in?"

"Yes, Michael." He rolled his eyes. "We've been through this a million times."

"I was thinking. What if we call you and leave it connected the whole time? You can put it in your front pocket. It'll make me feel better than us just sitting here wondering what's going on."

"As long as it's Josie's phone bill, not mine." Aleksander grinned like a kid playing cops and robbers, a game of pretend.

"And Alex. If you get the hint of anything being wrong. A gut feeling, even. Get out of there. You should stop here, don't want to be too close to the hotel."

Aleksander slowed down and parked up at the side of the road. "Relax. It's all good. Here you go." He passed Michael the keys to the car… just in case.

Michael held the keys in his hand, looking at them—the only belonging he now had. The fact that Alex would just hand them over to him, a basic stranger. He just couldn't make sense of it. Why did the people in this car trust him implicitly? What had he done to earn it? He looked at them both and smiled. The strange feeling that he would do anything for these people he had only known a few days was so intense it made him feel something he hadn't felt before, a sense of purpose, maybe. He tried to make sense of it.

"If we need to get away for any reason, we should agree a meeting place." Josie suggested, her hands clutched in front of her as if she was subconsciously praying.

"Don't worry." Aleksander dismissively waved his hand at them before getting out of the car. "Oh." He jumped a little as his phone buzzed in his chest pocket and he pulled it out, putting the phone to his ear. "Hello Josie." He waved to her through the window.

"Can you hear me?"

"Loud and clear. Over and out." He slipped the phone back in his pocket and saluted them, as he strode confidently in the direction of the hotel.

"Crazy son of a bitch." Michael said as he watched him disappear down the road.

"I can't believe he's doing this for us." Josie said as she put her phone on loud speaker so they could both hear.

It was too far to see the hotel, but Michael could see the churro man stood at his cart. His stomach protested at not having been fed for hours, but there was no way he could handle eating anything.

***

After about five minutes, they started to hear voices at the other end of the phone. They could only make out every other word. The speaker must have been muffled in his shirt pocket. Josie held the phone closer. A few rustling noises later, the voices became clearer.

"Do you have a locker for my stuff before I check in?" Josie stared at the phone as she listened as Aleksander's voice, surprisingly loud at the other end. Unfortunately, they couldn't make out any other voices. The next fifteen minutes crawled by painfully slowly. They couldn't hear anything at the other end of the phone except for clanging and rustling. Huddled around the phone in deep concentration, a knock at the window made Michael's heart skip a beat. The churro guy stood beaming through the glass at them.

Michael shrunk in his seat, wondering if the man had recognized him from the other day, but how could he? He and Josie looked completely different with their new haircuts and colors. Maybe this guy was just this friendly with everyone.

Josie opened the car door, and Michael's heart skipped a beat. The car was their safe space. As long as they stayed in the car, everything would be fine. Their protective cage of glass and metal. The ability to drive away in seconds. Why the hell was she drawing attention to herself? He watched the transaction. Josie shoved five pesos in his hand and grabbed a bag of warm churros. "Gracias." She thanked him and got back in the car.

"Calm down, Michael. We don't want to stand out. What could be more inconspicuous than two tourists tucking into some—"

Michael stopped her as he saw a figure rushing towards them. "Is that Alex already?" He squinted, trying to make them out as they got closer, tensed on the edge of his seat, waiting for a better view. He could make out the blue T-shirt Alex had been wearing. "It's him." Josie leaned to open the front door for him so he could slide in quickly. Aleksander's face was beet-red when he got to the car.

"Quick." He slid into the driver's seat and slammed the door shut behind him. "Keys!" He shouted.

"What's wrong?" Josie asked.

"Keys," he shouted again, louder this time. Alex was always so laid back, there was something deeply concerning about hearing him angry and panicked.

Michael tossed him the keys, but they fell into the footwell. Aleksander felt around on the floor, grabbing the key and putting it in the ignition. Once the engine started, he jerked forward, narrowly avoiding hitting the car in front before joining the road.

"Is everything okay?" Josie hunched forward, gripping the seat in front, bracing herself.

"See that Chevrolet?" He took his right hand off the steering wheel to point at a car at the end of the street.

"That's Julio's car." Michael and Josie turned to face each other with a mutual look of concern.

"Julio?" Aleksander glanced back at them.

"The hotel owner." Was the only information Michael wanted to give.

Alex slowed down to keep some space between them and the Chevrolet. "I thought Frederico run the hotel."

"No, that's his nephew."

"Well, I heard the nephew on the phone. Sounds like something big is going down. He mentioned a boat."

"Was there anything in the locker?" Despite everything going on, that bottle of Pentobarbital still meant more than anything.

Alex passed Michael a phone without taking his eyes off the other car. "This yours?"

"Holy crap." The phone was dead, but he recognized the deep scratch that took up most of the screen. He ran his finger over it.

"I couldn't see your bags. Place was so empty. Looked like it might be closing."

"Was there anything else?" Michael asked, trying to seem nonchalant, hiding his desperation.

"Your package? No. Sorry man."

"It's fine." He could probably buy more Pentobarbital somewhere else. Tijuana didn't have the monopoly on illicit substances, well it did, but there was still plenty to go around. "I don't think this is such a good idea. What if they notice us following them?"

"No worries. I'm the best covert driver." Alex bragged.

"Yeah, like when you almost crashed into the car in front a minute ago." Michael opened the small white bag and picked up a churro. The dough was still warm, and he ate it in two bites.

"That was intentional." Alex turned the corner.

"Yeah, I'm sure." Michael licked some sugar from his lips and sucked off the sticky oil from his fingers,

Once they had left Arelanes, they were back on the same highway they'd arrived on, back towards Chetumal. Alex made sure there was always at least one car between them at all times.

"So what are we doing exactly?" Michael asked, wondering what the hell was going through their minds.

"Maybe they lead us to Josie's sister." Alex shrugged. Michael hoped his unrelenting, enthusiastic optimism wouldn't rub off on Josie. Nothing good would come of this. They were in a downward spiral, spinning out of control. He had to get out before he was sucked in any further. After this he would not be going to the consulate. This was it. His money was almost gone, and he had little left to give.

"Quick, overtake this car. We're going to lose them." Josie fidgeted in the back seat with a nervous, excited energy—a newfound sense of purpose—practically buzzing. Alex complied and picked up speed to get ahead of the car in front. They were side by side and the other car matched Alex's speed. The gap had disappeared and Alex weaved a little towards the other lane.

"Careful. Last thing we want it to get arrested." Josie said as she looked over at Michael. He wondered if she could read his mind. Finally, the gap widened and Alex managed to ease his way in, with honks of protest from the other driver.

"Great. Very covert." Michael wasn't one to be a backseat driver, but this was getting painful to watch. He tried to dissociate, let whatever was going to happen, happen. He couldn't control any of it. He was a backseat driver to his own life, maybe even his own death.

They followed the Chevrolet past the small airport and towards the docks, past landmarks and shops that Michael recognized from when he had been in Julio's car.

"I wonder if they're going to Julio's boat." Josie thought out loud.

They drove past a road lined with bars and restaurants and followed the car left. A grassy island ran the length of the road, dotted with palms. The Chevrolet was directly in front of them now and slowed to a crawl.

"Why are they stopping? There's nothing here. They've seen us." Michael was used to being the voice of doom and gloom, but his ten dollar an hour student therapist wouldn't accuse him of catastrophizing now.

The car pulled up into the dusty layby in front of a chain-link fence that looked like it had seen better days. The conjoining gates were so bent the padlock was redundant. Anyone could slip through the gap. A large barren space, bar for a few heap-of-junk cars dotted around. The yard connected to a small auto-shop. A man with a shaved head sprinted from the garage with phone in hand and went to let the Chevrolet through the gates. Aleksander had no choice but to continue past them and pull around the corner. He parked as close as he could, right on the corner.

"What now, guys?" Alex stopped the engine in front of a small corrugated-iron construction tacked onto one of the main buildings.

Josie got out of the back of the car without saying a word and walked up to the wire fence beyond the property they parked in front of. As Michael followed, Alex got out and locked the car. She stood in front of the fence, watching.

"Can you see anything?" Alex leaned against the fence, curling his fingers around the wire.

"Can they see you?" Michael was tempted to yank them back.

"It's fine. We're miles away." She dismissed his concern with a wave of her hand.

"Slight exaggeration." He corrected her. Her complete

lack of concern was getting to him, unable to relate at all, as he worried about everything and everything. Whether he had left an appliance on would leave him anxious for hours. A job interview would make him feel sick to his stomach for days. Nothing seemed to faze Josie. It's as if the universe had taken all of her worry and gave it to him.

"Where are a pair of binoculars when you need them?" Her face pressed up against the metal, as close as she could get.

"Here." Alex jogged back to the car and from his backpack in the backseat, retrieved a compact, black pair of binoculars. He noticed the strange look Josie was giving him. "I like watching birds okay. Thought they might come in handy for this."

Josie eagerly snatched them from his hand and pointed them into the yard.

"I don't think we could be anymore obviou—"

"Shh! They've put something in the car. Big packs of something. Can't see." She adjusted the knob of the binoculars. "There's two guys. Shit. I can't be sure, but that guy—yep. That's Samuel. There's another guy."

Michael grabbed the binoculars and put his face up to the lenses, aiming through a gap in the fence—his worse fears confirmed. The image went blurry as the binoculars juddered in his shaking hands. He steadied himself again and saw Julio's nephew get back in the Chevrolet, and Samuel getting in a red Subaru. "They're leaving. Back in the car."

As they pulled back from the gate and turned to the car, they saw a man watching them from the auto-shop entrance. Michael's throat closed up as he walked towards them.

Chapter Twenty Six

"Can I help you?" This man was short and dumpy with a wide grin, about as nonthreatening as it got.

"Do you sell cars?" Alex swooped in with a charming smile. "It cost so much to rent here, y'know."

"Not really," the man said. "I only fix them. Now and then I buy for scrap but sometimes I end up fixing 'em up."

"Ah, okay. Thanks anyway." Alex headed to the car.

"If I have anything in, I let you know." The man held out a business card.

"That's great, thanks." Michael snapped up the card from his hand, eager to hurry this transaction along. "Los siento, we're in a hurry." Michael jumped in the back seat and Alex reversing, almost bumping the car behind.

"Not good." Michael slipped the business card into his pants pocket and tried to calm his trembling hands. "What if they know we're onto them?"

"It's okay. I thought Aleksander's cover story was

convincing enough. Quick thinking Alex. I like it." Josie wound her window down for some air.

***

"Can someone please just tell me what we're trying to accomplish here?" Michael had no idea where they were now, but they continued to tail Samuel's car, regardless. On the lonelier stretches of road, they almost lost sight of it. Idiots, was the word that kept popping into Michael's head as the humidity molded itself around his skin like cling-film, clogging his pores. He could see the newspaper headline now: Three tourists found dead in the jungle.

The thick cover of trees on each side of the road grew sparse, revealing open spaces of thick lush grass, and the road changed from bumpy gravel to smooth light-gray tarmac. The Subaru turned into a driveway. Michael got a glimpse up the long drive as they drove past and found somewhere for them to stop. "Not too close," he said, looking for somewhere with a bit of cover. They couldn't park out in the open, so continued to a single-lane road that ran parallel to the drive. Gentle landscaped slopes rose and fell between the two roads.

"Looks like a golf course." Josie looked out at the man-made hills. "We need to get closer. I wonder if they have security?"

It occurred to him to verbalize how crazy this was, but knew it wouldn't do any good. When the car came to a stop, it was eerily quiet and Josie reached for the door handle. "Wait." He put his arm out as if going to stop her. "What's the plan here?" for once, he felt like the sane one.

"We're just going to have a look."

"A look?" He parroted her words back to her, hoping she would realize how ridiculous they sounded.

"Yeah. A look." The firmness in her voice solidified the fact that there would be no talking her out of this.

"And then what? Get arrested for trespassing? Get shot? What happened to going to the consulate? Now that was a plan I could get behind."

"It'll be fine." She uttered. It was basically the equivalent of, because I said so. There was no arguing, rationalizing, or reasoning.

"Have you got amnesia or something? Have the last few days just slipped your mind?" He couldn't conceal his frustration much longer. He wanted Josie and Alex safe. He wanted to be back in his hotel room more than anything.

"We'll be careful. We won't get too close. Just scope it out." She went to open the car door, and Michael stopped her.

"Why don't you two stay in the car. I will check it out. Just me." If this was going to happen, he might as well implement some damage control.

"I'm going with you," she stated emphatically.

"One person would be less noticeable." That wasn't the reason he insisted on going alone, and he could tell she knew it too.

"Then I will go alone." She opened the door and swung it open.

"Like hell you are." He grabbed her shoulder.

"She's MY sister."

"It's not like she's going to be here. She's long gone." He shut up as soon as he saw her jaw clench.

"Oh so tell me, big strong man, if I weren't a woman, would you have a problem with me going?"

"What are you even talking about? I don't want Alex going either."

"Woah. Cool it." Alex shouted, as if addressing two children arguing over a toy. Michael half expected to be put in time-out. "I stay with the car. Just do it quickly. Have a look. Come straight back. I'll be waiting."

"Fine." Michael conceded. "But there's something I have to do first.

Chapter Twenty Seven

Alex watched Michael with curiosity as he loaded up the camera on his phone and pressed the record button.

"Hello. My Name is Michael Ashton, and I am here with Josie Quinn. If anything happens to us, we want the truth to be known. Josie's sister—Tanya, was kidnapped in the Quinta Roo region of Mexico a year ago." His dry throat felt like it was closing up, trying to stop him from continuing, but he coughed and carried on. "She was never found. I've been helping her sister try to find out what happened and here is what we know so far. We know the kidnapper was named Ismael Garcia, and that he was paid by Samuel Valentino Hernandez to do so. Why, this remains unclear, but we know it has something to do with someone nicknamed El Verdugo." It just occurred to Michael he was speaking like a TV news-anchor, but somehow it seemed more fitting. "Samuel Hernandez attempted to kill us, but we got away with the help of Miguel Cuevas, whose wife was brutally murdered by Samuel. Miguel was with us when she was killed." Michael didn't know what else to say and looked towards Josie. "Do you want to leave a message for your family? Just in case?" He passed her the phone to hold, and she held it in front of her, pausing for a few seconds. Her eyes became glassy, as if it just hit her that she may never see them again.

"Hi mom. Dad. I know you said you didn't want me to do this, and I'm so sorry if I don't come back. I never meant to make this harder on you." Her voice cracked, and she breathed in deeply before beginning her next sentence. "I hope you understand why I did what I did, and I'm still glad I did it. I am so close now to knowing what happened. I can't give up now. I'm just imagining me home, maybe Tanya is even there. It's Thanksgiving, and mom, you always insist on buying the biggest turkey you can find, even though we never get through all the leftovers. And dad, you always pass out with a glass of wine in your hand before midnight. It was always one of the few times in the year that Tanya would actually be at home, mainly because no-where else would be open." She laughed for a second, then stopped herself, and passed the phone back to Michael without saying another word, and got out of the car. He saved the recording and messaged it to Alex.

"You know what to do. If anything does happen, don't hesitate; get the hell out of here. Wish me luck." They shared a heavy, half smile.

"You're not going to need it." Alex said with confidence.

Alex's words bounced around Michael's head as he went to follow Josie. 'You're not going to need it.' Why the hell would he say that? Oh well. Fate had been tempted now, and there was no turning back.

The air was still enough that they could hear the rustling of grass underfoot as they made their way towards where Samuel had gone. Once over the first hump they tried to stick to dips in the bumpy landscape to avoid being seen. A row of trees provided them cover as they walked alongside the drive. It must have been a good half a mile before they could make out the house in the distance—a tall three story, reflecting the light with its pristine white walls, sparkling green pool, and glass doors. Modern—a miniature version of something you might see in the Hollywood hills, only instead of sprawling across the land, it towered up into the sky—a white beacon in this distance. The base of the house nestled in carefully manicured foliage and spindly palm trunks almost as tall as the building itself. As they got closer, they could make out two figures on the terrace.

Michael considered one last word of caution, but thought

it best to remain silent.

As they waited in the shade of the palms, Michael pulled pieces of lint away from his pocket. It was a strangely calming activity, but he moved onto tearing the business card in his pocket into fours. Keeping his hands busy took his mind away from what was happening. Self-soothing.

"Give me that." She took the pieces of torn card from his hand. "You know, tearing things up is a sign of sexual frustration."

He couldn't believe she was making jokes right now, but mustered a half-smile.

Josie laid the pieces onto the grass, placing them together like a jigsaw puzzle. "No way." She got onto her knees and inspected the card closer.

"What?" He whispered. They were far enough away that he probably didn't have to keep his voice down, but he wasn't taking any chances.

"Didn't Miguel say his business partner that Samuel hired to kidnap my sister was called Ismael?"

"Yeah, Ismael Garcia. Garcia like the ice cream." He would have killed from some cooling ice-cream at that moment.

"Oh, my god." She picked up the scraps of card from the floor and thrust them into his hand. "It's his auto-shop. The scum bag that kidnapped my sister was the guy that gave us his card."

Michael arranged the pieces to see the name Ismael Garcia in smudged black ink.

"This is it, Michael. We're so close now."

"Josie." Michael leaped from the ground, putting his hands up in a defensive stance as a man stood approaching from behind Josie with an AK-47 in his arms. An unintelligible noise escaped his mouth as he flinched in anticipation of pain, but the man didn't fire. With her back to him, Josie's hand disappeared into the pocket of her tailored shorts, and her phone almost slipped from her hand as she pulled it out. The voice in Michael's head screamed for her to stop, but her fingers started pushing buttons. The man shouted words he didn't understand, but he knew they weren't good.

"Leave! Now." Josie shouted down the phone. "Get help."

Before Michael could react, the man struck her across the back of the head, sending her phone flying into the grass as her body dropped to the floor in an instant. "Please." Michael uttered. He wasn't use to begging for his life.

As he felt a presence behind him and a shadow appeared at his side, Michael's organs leapt up inside him.

"You took your time. Trouble finding the place?" Samuel's gravelly voice rasped near his ear, close enough so he could feel the heat of his breath. A loud noise, like a car backfiring in the distance, made Michael flinch.

"What is that?" Samuel yelled and Michael couldn't tell if he was talking to him, or the man with the machine gun.

"I… don't… know." He stuttered. The sound still rang, bouncing off the hills from the direction of the car where Alex was waiting for them and Michael's stomach churned. He clenched his fists, fighting the urge to vomit. His body screamed, confused, not sure whether it wanted to run, throw up, cry, or curl up into a ball.

"Never mind. I'm sure Che is dealing with it." He gave the man with the gun a knowing look and he hoisted Josie up, pulling her along whilst carrying the gun over the other shoulder. Samuel looked at Michael. "Move it. You've got legs, right?"

The turquoise pool reflected in the glass panels of the ground floor doors as they neared the house and stepped up onto the paving. Despite the expansive windows, the trees that surrounded the property provided plenty of privacy. Even though he could barely think straight, he couldn't help but be overwhelmed by the lavishness of the place and he felt like he was locked in an architect's wet-dream. It reminded him of the real-estate shows he'd watch at midday when he was unemployed. Never in his life had he stepped foot in somewhere like this. The fully white interior, glass staircase and shiny floors were dazzling. Although the floor space hadn't looked like much in comparison to the height of the house, the inside was vast, the open plan floor, designed to make optimal use of the space. Despite the wow-factor, the place felt sterile. No nick-knacks, no photographs, nothing to make it look like a home. An enormous television and sound system took up one wall, and a highly stylized artwork hung on the opposing wall. Minimalist bright colors that ultimately didn't make you feel anything when you looked at them.

The back part of the ground floor was raised up from the rest, and Samuel led them up to a bar area. A curved granite counter with various liqueur's laid out and a row of pristine glasses. A charcoal-gray chaise lounge took up the other half of the space. "Sit."

The armed man slumped Josie up against the backrest, and Michael placed himself gingerly on the edge of one of the cushions.

"Playlist three," Samuel said, and in a second classical music blasted from the speakers. "Blinds down." As soon as he said it, a mechanical whirring started as a covering came down from above the front doors and windows, lowering slowly like a garage door, and the house grew dim as the sunlight disappeared bit-by-bit. "Cool, no?" He grinned, baring perfectly straight, white teeth. Pleased with himself like a teenage boy who had gotten his hands on the latest gaming console. Michael shuffled on the edge of his seat. What was Samuel waiting for? Why didn't he just kill them already and get it over with? It was the waiting that was excruciating.

The other guy laid his gun out on the bar and answered his phone, talking a mile-a-minute, pacing up and down—a caged lion in a zoo enclosure—frustrated and unpredictable. Michael couldn't bring himself to look at their faces, so concentrated on the tattoos on the man's arms, his eyes following the lines and patterns.

The man then relayed whatever was said on the phone to Samuel. The words were foreign to Michael, but the volume and tone didn't inspire him with confidence. Anger always sent his heart-rate soaring. In all his years of working in customer service, he could never get used to it. Josie groaned at his side as she started to come around. He wished he could reach out to her, but didn't dare move.

A projectile hurtled towards the back wall. He hadn't even realized what it was until the glass bottle exploded against the wall, leaving liquid dripping down the walls and shards of glass firing in every direction. Something had seriously pissed

Samuel off, and he strode towards them, shoving a phone towards him.

"You call your friend. Tell him to get back here now. Don't you dare tell him anything is wrong. Tell him whatever you need to tell him to get his ass back here."

"Who?" he stammered and looked over at Josie, who looked confused and held her hand against her head, where she had been struck.

"Your driver. Don't play dumb with me, you little shit-stain. Stop looking at her. Look at me when I'm talking to you."

"I… I."

Samuel yanked Michael's arm back, nearly ripping it from its socket, and leaving him struggling for breath. "Call him. Now, or I'll tear your girlfriend a new one, literally." He let go of his arm and took a step back, dropping the phone on the cushion. Begging his body to co-operate, Michael scrolled through Josie's contact list. The words were a blur and might as well have been hieroglyphics. His fingers felt numb and tingly, like they were not part of him, but he finally managed to find Alex's number and pressed the bright green dial button.

"Speakerphone!" Samuel demanded, but Michael could barely function enough to find the right button. The phone went straight to voice-mail.

"Don't leave a message. We will try again in a minute."

He wandered over to the bar, poured a large measure of some see-through liquor in two thick glass tumblers, pulled some ice from a mini-fridge and threw it unceremoniously into the glasses. He came to Michael and shoved a glass in his hand. The ice-cubes chinked against the glass as Michael's hands trembled. It took a monumental amount of effort to keep the glass still, so he used both hands to steady it. He looked down at the white bubbles of air trapped in the ice-cubes.

"Drink. It's good stuff. You'll enjoy." He took a sip from his glass, his hands calm and steady. Samuel swayed from side to side with the music like he didn't have a care in the world, or he was putting on some show. Being up on this platform made Michael feel like he was on stage. This wasn't real; it couldn't be.

Josie finally sat upright in a groggy daze. He could only imagine what was going through her head right now.

"Ah, sleeping beauty. Let me get you a drink. Gotta say, love the blonde hair."

"Please, just tell me what happened to Tanya. That's all I ask."

"Let me do the asking first." He passed her a glass, and

she took it obligingly. "You speak to your friend. Get him back here. Then we talk."

"Give me the phone." Her arm stretched out; her hand open.

He dropped the phone in her hand, not taking his eyes away from hers.

She held the phone up to her ear and waited. "Hey. Alex. If you get this message, don't worry. Everything's fine. False alarm. We're stuck here though. We need a ride back to town." The slow and steady timbre of her voice was so calm Michael almost believed it.

Samuel took the phone back straight after the call. "Good girl."

"My sister?"

"You'll find out when your friend comes back, and only then."

They sat in quiet contemplation. Michael couldn't believe Josie's cold voice message, like she had no qualms with endangering an innocent to get the truth. As if the truth was the only thing that mattered in the world, everyone else be damned. She could make her own decisions. Michael didn't fear death, but lying to Aleksander didn't sit right with him. The mournful sounds of the piano from the speakers made him feel like he was a star in his own movie, destined for a tragic ending. He hoped Alex would have some sense and stay away.

"Let's go outside," Samuel said, with a frenetic energy, bobbing up and down like a dog waiting for their owner to take them out for a walk. He was excited for something, and Michael didn't want to know what.

Chapter Twenty Eight

The dusk had painted the sky lilac by the time they went outside. Michael hadn't expected it to be getting dark already, but his grasp on time had slipped. Everything looked so much more beautiful at twilight, and his mind drifted back to the beautiful sunset he had witnessed at the petrified waterfall near Oaxaca. This would likely be his last view.

The stark silhouettes of the palm trees cut into the sky, which had now darkened into a deep magenta. Samuel walked in front, making his way up white steps up the terraced garden, and the man with the machine gun was behind them. At the end of the main part of the garden was a huge circular fire-pit made of pale brick.

The colors above the tree-line seemed to change every few seconds and he couldn't take his eyes off it. The knowledge that it was probably his last sunset made him focus on every nuance—the way the burnt-orange clouds feathered into the stratosphere.

"You still with us." Samuel clicked his fingers in front of Michael's face. "Here, take this. You need it more than I do." He passed Michael his drink and went to fetch something from his right-hand man. He dropped the hefty bags onto the ground in front of Josie and Michael. The knock-off North Face backpack and Josie's dark purple luggage was instantly recognizable—their bags from the hotel. "Let's see what we have here." Samuel leaned down, starting with her bag. He unzipped it slowly, as if he was trying to build up tension. He pulled out a dress and held it up to himself. "Hm, I don't think this would suit me." He tossed it into the fire pit as the man—still armed—went to work to get a fire going.

There was already wood in the pit, and he dowsed it with a liberal squirt of gasoline. The smell stung Michael's nostrils, and a white flash of light blinded him as the gas combusted. Michael blinked as the flames subsided enough so he could see. "Hm, boring, boring." Samuel threw various items of clothing in the fire indiscriminately. Embers floated up into the sky before fading into white dots of ash and then disappearing entirely. The fabric fed the flames and the pile of clothes started shrinking in on itself as it burned, like a body decomposing in fast-forward.

Next, he pulled out her makeup bag and chucked it straight in the fire, then toiletries. The fire expanding with a whoosh as something fueled the flames. "See. It's like you never existed."

"You know, the police are probably coming here now. Alex would have told them. You really want to have them stumble upon this? You'll go down for this. If you let us go… I swear we won't tell anyone." Josie pleaded.

"I doubt it." He unzipped the small pocket at the front of the bag and pulled out her passport. "Lastly, but most importantly." He opened her passport at the photo page and held it up next to her face before adding it to the rest of her burning belongings. He added the whole bag to the fire and watched as it popped and crackled. "There's something about fire, don't ya think, something primal." No-one responded or said a word after that for a good five minutes, transfixed by the fire as the bag started disintegrating, making room for whatever was next.

Shadows danced across Josie's face, her eyes glistening in the orange light as she watched her things disappear into the fiercely rising and falling flames. She swallowed hard, and Michael wondered if she was holding back tears. As Samuel started on Michael's bag, he felt nothing. His limited personal-effects meant nothing to him. It wasn't the reaction Samuel wanted, and he looked pissed off as he kept checking Michael's face for a reaction. "Okay, now that's over with.

There's one more thing missing." Miguel's right-hand man passed him a small bottle as if he and Samuel had rehearsed this moment. Samuel held the bottle up to the light emanating from the fire. "What's this, Michael? You left it in your locker. You must have wanted to keep it safe."

"That's not mine." He coughed, the thick smoke catching in his throat.

"Come on. Michael. We both know that's not true. So tell us, what is it?" Something in Samuel's expression told Michael he already knew full well what it was.

"It's nothing." Michael said, knowing already that Samuel would just keep pushing, and wondered what he should say.

"What were you doing with it then?" He paced in front of the fire, the flames licking him from behind. "Why are you here, Michael? Tell us. I'm interested."

"Fine." He could tell Samuel wouldn't let this go. "I came here to get Pentobarbital. I came here to die." It felt strange finally saying those words to another person. No-one ever knew he'd had these thoughts, not that there was really anyone to tell.

"You came here to die?" A smirk twitched at one corner of Samuel's mouth.

"Yes. I came here to kill myself." He looked down at the paving slabs, unable to rid the shame from his voice. The words hung awkwardly—their implication suspended in the silence without response—met only by the roar of the fire.

Finally, someone spoke. Josie shuffled towards him just a little. "You should have said someth—"

"So you're a man with nothing to lose." Samuel's smirk turned downwards. "In order words, dangerous." He stoked the fire with a metal implement, making sure the remnants of everything would be consumed. "I've got my eye on you Michael." He led them back to the house, leaving the fire to burn.

Chapter Twenty Nine

They watched in silence as Samuel poured himself another drink and snorted a line of cocaine off of the granite countertop of the bar. "So, I was thinking. How best to deal with you two." He sniffed and rubbed his nose. "My man Che here likes to keep things simple, quick. But where's the fun in that? This guy has no imagination." He playfully elbowed the man, who continued to stand straight, holding his gun. His expression unchanging. "Then it occurred to me." He went back to the counter to have another line. Michael couldn't bring himself to look at Josie as they sat, planted to their seats. "You know what?" He approached Josie slowly, and she flinched as he tucked a tendril of bleach-blonde hair behind her ear. "You look just like her, you know. Younger and hotter, though. I bet he can't wait to meet you. He always liked a younger-model. Don't we all?"

"Who?" Josie's voice wavered as her lip quivered ever so slightly.

"You're playing dumb again. El Verdugo." He sat down next to her and leaned in closer, resting one hand on Josie's thigh, and slipped his other arm around her shoulder, his hand loosely holding his drink. "When Che told him you were in town... wow... his face. You should have seen it." He noticed Josie transfixed on his hand placed on her leg that shook underneath. He laughed as he noticed her discomfort and took his hands off her. "You think I would? I'm not a monster." He got up from the seat. "Anyway, I need to deal with your boyfriend first."

"So, I was thinking, how should I dispose of you. Then it came to me. Give the man what he wants. Everyone wins. What do you say, Michael?" He grabbed the bottle of pentobarbital and shook it. "Less messy. You want to leave a good-looking corpse, right?"

Michael looked at the bottle in Samuel's hand. It was the best thing that could happen to him. Relatively painless. He could just fall asleep. Not have to deal with this hell he was currently in, but couldn't imagine leaving Josie alone in that hell, not by choice. Before he knew what was happening Che restrained him from behind as Samuel unscrewed the bottle. "Not to be cliche, but do you want to do this the easy way, or the hard way?"

It crossed Michael's mind that they could be safe at the American Embassy right now. If he could just go back in time, he would have made sure of it.

"No." He tugged his arms trying to pull them from Che's vice like grasp

"Fine. I tried to play nice." He pinched Michael's nose in between his fingers, squeezing his nostrils so no air could get through. "Just open your mouth. Easy."

Michael had never been able to hold his breath for long and knew it would only be a matter of time before he would have to open his mouth.

"Everyone is always the same. They think they'll go out like a man. They think they're brave. But when it comes down to it, they just can't face their own death. They beg, and they beg. This one guy even pissed himself. Like some little kid." He chuckled. "You wouldn't have done it. You would have pussied out."

The feeling of being unable to breathe was indescribable. It wasn't pain per se. Discomfort. Yet somehow, it was so visceral. His cheeks flushed red-hot as every cell of his body screamed for oxygen. His body started shaking. It happened, his mouth opened like a floodgate to let the air stream in and in that second, Samuel rammed the neck of the glass bottle into his mouth and tried to tip Michael's head back as Che tightened his grip. The bitter liquid attacked his taste-buds making him gag.

Chapter Thirty

Before he even knew what was going on, Samuel pulled back and the bottle smashed against the hard floor. Josie hung off of Samuel, her arm wrapped around his neck. He ripped her off of his back and slammed her onto the floor with the precision and ease of a professional wrestler.

"Oh, Josie." He stood above her, watching her struggle on the floor. "Maybe it was you I should have been keeping an eye on." Che released Michael from his grip and approached Josie. He had switched to a handgun and pointed it down at her.

"Never mind. I was trying to do you a favor. I guess it's time to get out of here." Samuel disappeared to the front of the house, leaving them both with Che. Josie had got up from the floor and stood—stuck to the spot. "Did you miss me?" He came back with cable-ties and span Josie around and secured the plastic around her wrists. He chucked another cable-tie over to Che who grabbed Michael, slipped the tie over his hands and yanked it tight enough to make Michael wince, and within a minute it felt like his circulation was being cut off. He could feel the pulse beating, twitching, trying to get blood to his numb fingers. Che grabbed Michael's pinkie finger and wrenched it, snapping it to the side, unleashing an agonized scream from Michael's throat that drowned out the music blaring from the speakers. The intense pain ripped through him, bringing him to his knees.

***

They marched from the house into the night. As insects chirped and trees rustled, they followed the path to Samuel's car. There was no use running. They were slower, weaker, and unarmed. They wouldn't stand a chance. All they could do was let Samuel dictate their every action. An image slipped into Michael's head. He imagined slamming Samuel's head against the car, and pounding it into the metal again and again and again, until his face was nothing but a slippery, bloody mush. Somehow the thought made him feel better.

A weird sense of calm and drowsiness washed over him and wondered if the small amount of pentobarbital he had ingested had something to do with it. They were forced into the back of the car and told not to cause any trouble. The engine started, and the headlights flared into the darkness of the road in front. The low purr of the engine and the rocking movement as the car started was soothing, lulling, taking away the harshness of the outside world and into the cocoon of his mind.

"Michael." Josie nudged him with her knee.

"What?" He widened his eyes to try to counteract the sleepiness that tried to take over him.

"Are you okay?" She whispered.

"Brilliant. Why do you ask?" He was surprised he was able to muster sarcasm in his current state.

"Why didn't you tell me you were going to—"

"It doesn't even matter now." He interrupted her. He didn't want to talk about it. The way people talked about stuff like this made him cringe. People would go all high pitched like they were talking to a three-year-old.

Samuel's eyes narrowed as he eyed them up through the rear-view mirror. "You better not be conspiring back there."

Josie stopped talking, and Michael was almost glad. He wasn't ready for this conversation. This is why he never told anyone in the first place. He was certain he would hear the standard platitudes: but there's so much to live for, you can't appreciate the good without the bad, permanent solution to a temporary problem. He agreed to the latter point in part. It was a permanent solution, hence its appeal. He disagreed, however, with the temporary problem part. What the fuck did they know? Just because life was easy for them. What right did they have to try to force him to continue living? They didn't have to live his life, and he was certain, if they had, they would be singing a different tune. Michael bounced up in his chair, with no seatbelt to secure him, or free hands to steady himself. The bumps in the road tossed him around. The headlights of another car came from the opposite side of the road, and for a microsecond, he considered trying to get their attention, but if he tried, it wouldn't end well. His head felt heavy, like a bowling ball balanced on his neck, gravity willing it to roll right off. He tried to lean back against the headrest, but his hands behind his back made it difficult. His hands were completely numb now like they had been dunked in ice-water, in contrast to his arms which pulsated with a burning sensation from being bent back in such an awkward position. Instead, he leaned his head to the side. It hammered against the window with every bump in the road, but he was too tired to care. He wondered if he cared about any of it anymore. None of this was his responsibility. The only thing that he wanted in that moment, was to close his eyes. Unfortunately, that wouldn't come to pass as Josie opened her mouth.

"Why do you do what you do?" She asked. It sounded half

like an accusation, half like genuine curiosity.

Samuel took a moment to formulate a response, his dark-eyed glare burning through them. "Why everyone does it. Money."

"Money. That's it? Why kidnap my sister, was that just for money? If so, why didn't you release her?"

"Hey. It wasn't up to me. Besides, you're right. Sure, It's about money. It ain't like wherever the fuck you live in some bubble. Don't think I didn't notice your designer clothes. What did you do to earn that? Ask mommy and daddy? But yeah, it's not just about money. You ever feel alive in your bubble, Josie? I know you. I could see it in your eyes. You're loving this. A little bit of excitement. You have some serious balls, my friend. Got tired of your small boring life, coming to taste some of the danger. It's intoxicating, isn't it?"

"You're wrong." She protested.

He carried on talking, ignoring her comment. "There's nothing quite fucking like it. Kill or be killed. Watching someone go from the enemy, to just a hunk of meat. Watching them cower. The respect you get. It's fucking primal. Some next level god-like shit. I mean seriously, can you imagine a world without crime? That's some mundane bull-shit. Boring." He pulled a right, they drove for a few minutes, and he picked up where he had left off. "I heard once why people like horror films. The adrenaline they get. The threat of death, it's like an aphrodisiac. They did a study on it and everything. People like bumping uglies after watching them. It's like the danger gets them off. Apparently it's some biological thing. Survival instinct. If your body thinks it's going to die, it makes you want to make babies before you go. Funny, no?" He chuckled to himself before making another turn.

Michael wasn't convinced by his theory and remained silent.

"We're almost here." They drove another few miles down a lonely stretch of road, devoid of other cars until another set of headlights appeared in the distance. A blasting smash made Michael's heart stop, and he ducked as the windshield shattered into a million pieces, showering Samuel and Che in glass fragments. A screech cut through the air as the car veered to the side. They lost control. His body was thrown around like a theme park ride. Chest pounding. His muscles tensed as he tried to brace himself. No idea which way was up. Finally, the world stopped moving and everything went still, and then black.

Chapter Thirty One

The sensation of falling jolted Michael awake. Had he been dreaming? It was quiet except for a hissing coming from somewhere as he tried to get his bearings. His hands still tied behind his back and his chest resting against the roof of the car, which was now facing the floor as the car laid upside down. Glass everywhere. A movement against him made him flinch, and he wriggled just enough that he could crane his neck and see Josie stirring. With his hands bound, he couldn't touch her, couldn't help.

The window next to him had blown out, an escape hatch to freedom, and he inched towards it like a Caterpillar crawling across the floor. His head emerged through the gap and he looked around. It was so dark he could barely see a thing. His head throbbed with a pulsating pain, like the worst hangover of his life, but he fought the urge to give up and just lay there and forged forward, leaning his elbow against the frame of the window and propelling himself forward with his legs. A sharp-hot sensation dragged across his arm as he rolled out onto the damp grass. He lay on the floor gasping with the effort and looked at his arm. A long, deep-red gash ran along it, and warm wet blood trickled from the wound and dripped onto the floor. It made him queasy, so he opted to stop looking at it and pretend it didn't exist.

"Get me out of here." Josie's weak voice came from the car.

"I don't know how?" He tried to prize his hands apart with pure strength alone, knowing it wouldn't work, but trying anyway.

"Listen to me." Josie said. "Stand up."

He did what he was told and made his way to his knees. Every muscle in his body felt weak, and it took a surprising amount of effort to right himself without his hands to balance. He looked to see if there was a sharp bit of exposed metal he could use to cut the plastic.

"Just bring your hands up as high as you can and drop them down really hard." Her voice was stronger now. Michael did what she said, but nothing happened. "It might take a few tries, but it will happen."

"How do you know?" He wondered if she was having him on, but he couldn't imagine her joking at a time like this.

"I did some research before I came. You know, just in

case. Do it already."

"Just in case you were bound with cable ties?" His mind was bracing itself for this not to work. He considered cutting the tie apart with the glass in the window frame but didn't want to injure himself again.

"Hurry up." She shouted.

He strained to get his hands up as high as possible and swung them down again. Nothing. This was useless.

"Again." She yelled in encouragement.

This time, something clicked. He hadn't even realized it worked at first. Not quite believing his hands were free, as he couldn't feel them. He held them up in front of him.

"Michael," she shouted from the car.

He ran around to her side and pulled on the door, but it wouldn't open. "You're going to have to come out of the window I came out of. You have to be real careful through. I cut myself." He pulled the protruding dagger of glass that he had cut himself on from the frame, before easing her towards him. He used the shard of glass to cut her cable tie so she could get out easier, making sure not to shred fingers in the process. She crawled out the window towards him and he put his arms around her as she caught her breath, before going to check to see what became of Samuel and Che. They couldn't hear them. Michael crouched down in front of the driver's window. Samuel was gone. He could see Che hanging from his seat-belt. Blood dripped from his head onto the roof of the car. It looked like the exit wound of a gunshot.

"He's gone." Michael said, watching gray smoke billowing up from the car.

"Shit." Josie backed away from a rustling sound, and the figure of a man came down from the roadside. Michael and Josie sprinted in the opposite direction towards tree cover. Maybe this was their chance.

"Stop. It's me."

Michael stopped in his tracks. "Miguel?" No other words would come to him. He had no idea what to say after what had happened.

"Where is he?"

"Who? Samuel. We don't know. He must have ran off." Michael looked in all directions, but it was so dark all he could make out was the shifting shadows of trees swaying.

"What are you doing here?" Michael still couldn't believe he was here. In the middle of nowhere. Part of him wondered if his own body was still in the car wreck, unconscious, dreaming. He was having an out-of-body experience. "Did you shoot the car? My memories a bit fuzzy."

"Yes. I came to find you. I was pretty sure Samuel would have taken you here."

"Why what is here?" Michael asked, but Miguel didn't answer. Michael wasn't sure he wanted to know the answer anyway. "We can get in your car, get out of here."

"Not without him. Samuel will die tonight. I'm not going to let him get away with it."

"I'm so sorry. We feel awful. If it wasn't for us."

"Samuel is a psycho. One step wrong and he may have done what he did anyway. The families he's done it to before." Miguel looked like he was going to say something else, but stopped himself.

"We saw you get arrested. How are you here right now?" Josie asked, looking as surprised as Michael felt.

"They knew the whole thing was a farce. They had nothing. They had to let me out."

"What are you going to do?" Josie asked, taking charge of the conversation.

"Find him."

"But he could be anywhere by now." She reasoned.

"I'm going to check around here. He must be injured. He can't be far. You take Josie to my car. It's parked up there." He tossed his keys to Michael and didn't give him time to answer before he traipsed towards the woods. Yet another person entrusted Michael with their car and assumed that Michael could drive. He passed the keys to Josie, and they started up the incline towards the road. "I'm worried about Alex. What if he goes back to Samuel's?"

"He won't." Her casual tone bothered him.

"How can you be so sure?" He wasn't looking forward to broaching this.

"Last night. I think you were already in bed. Me and Alex came up with a safe phrase for when he was checking out the hotel. If he was in any trouble, I told him to say the safe phrase. We came up with something that wouldn't be obvious that he could say if he was in trouble, that wouldn't draw attention, like if he was kidnapped or something."

"What?"

"False alarm. I told him to say it was a false alarm. Although the tables were turned, I'm sure he knew not to come."

"Thank fuck for that." Everything started to make sense now. How she could have been so calm. "So is he going to call the police? They must know we're missing by now."

"Um, yeah. Probably not." She grimaced.

"Why not?"

"He told me that he's overstayed his visa. He doesn't want to get into trouble."

"Yeah but, that's not life and death." Michael felt a little hurt.

"I don't know." The slope started to flatten out as they reached the road. Miguel's car was pulled up at side. Even in the dark they could make out the black skid-marks from where Samuel's car had lost control. The open road felt empty and exposed. Michael scanned the area, but there was no-one, just black road stretching into the darkness until it disappeared.

They hurried across the road to Miguel's car and got inside. They didn't know whether to turn on the engine, have the car ready to go, or whether that would draw more attention to themselves.

"Miguel could have easily got us killed when he shot at the car." Josie mused, pulling down the sun-visor and glancing in the small mirror. "Wow. I look like shit."

"He's hell-bent on getting Samuel. Understandable given the circumstances." Michael fixated on the dash-light that Josie had switched on. "You two have that in common." He flicked off the light switch and watched Josie blindly rummage around the glove compartment to keep herself occupied.

"I wonder how long we're going to have to wait here. We're sitting ducks." Michael shifted in his chair. "We can't leave Miguel though, so I guess we're stuck here. If only we had a weapon or something."

"Like this?" Josie pulled a massive handgun from the glove box.

"Fuck." Michael blurted, taken aback.

"Do you know how to use that?"

"How hard could it be?" She joked as she inspected the firearm. "Listen, Michael. I'm sorry about back at Samuel's. You were looking out for me and I know I'm stubborn."

"It's okay," he said, hoping this wouldn't turn into a conversation about the pentobarbital Samuel had found in his luggage. "You look like a bad-ass with that thing," he tried changing the subject.

"When we get back to town, I'm going to the consulate. Do this the right way," Josie said. Michael breathed a sigh of relief and noticed her eyes fixed on him. "What are you going to do after?" she asked coyly, but he could tell she was fishing to find out if he planned on following through with his plan to end his life.

"I don't know." The niggling doubts had already started working their way into his psyche.

"I hate the thought of not seeing you again after all this, but I don't want to be a hypocrite. I feel like people are always going to do what they're going to do. Like me. I've done stupid things. Reckless things, and no-one was ever going to talk me out of them." There wasn't even a hint of judgement in her voice. "I wish you wouldn't though. Just want you to know that." They sat in the car in silence for a minute. It wasn't awkward, but it wasn't comfortable either—just limbo.

Josie leaned across, resting her head on Michael's shoulder while he watched the road ahead, glancing behind him every now and then. Maybe Samuel was injured and lying in the forest somewhere, bleeding out—one could only hope. She placed her hand on his chest, and he became increasingly aware of his heart pounding—a tight ball of adrenaline and tension thumping under his ribcage. He wondered if she could feel it too. He could see the movement of her chest rising and falling from the corner of his eye, and she looked directly into his eyes. It was a moment he recognised, that moment just before, when both of you know what's going to happen, that micro-second that feels like it goes on for minutes.

Their lips met instinctively, lightly at first, and then firmer and more urgently. They pressed up against each other and he put his hand through her hair, and rested it behind her head, his other hand against her back. This was insane, Michael thought. Samuel could be there any minute and shoot them dead in a heart-beat, yet he couldn't stop himself. In that moment, this was all that mattered. Her hands wandered under his shirt, touching his bare skin. It felt so good being close to someone, like everything else could go to hell around them and it wouldn't matter. Josie let out a moan and their movements became frenzied. Maybe Samuel had been right about death and sex. Every touch felt heightened with crazed hormones racing through them.

Something didn't feel right. He pulled away.

"What's wrong?" A look of concern spread across her flushed face.

"Shit." He pushed Josie down as he saw a figure in front of the car. "Where's the gun?"

"I don't know." She scrabbled about, frantically trying to locate where she had put the gun. The side window shattered and a deafening noise rang in his ears. He hunched over, holding his arms over his head, as glass fragments fell from his back.

"Get out the car." Samuel shouted from the broken side window. Michael berated himself for allowing himself to get distracted. He tentatively opened the door and inched out slowly, avoiding making any sudden movements. "Now pass me that gun, Josie. Trust me —before you could fire a shot —Michael's brains will be splattered all over this car."

She complied straight away. Michael wanted to yell at her just to shoot Samuel. It didn't matter what happened to him.

Giving his life to end Samuel's seemed like a good trade. Josie would be safe. Michael would be at peace. It was a win-win. He couldn't get a word out, as everything seemed to happen so fast.

"Get in the back." Samuel demanded and watched Michael open the door, keeping his gun on him. Michael wondered if Josie would have time to start up the engine and drive off before Samuel managed to get in the car—he doubted it.

"Where is Miguel?" he shouted as he got in the front passenger seat.

"I don't know. I really don't know. He just told us to wait here and went looking for you." Michael said, vaguely comforted by the knowledge that at least Miguel was still alive.

"I'll have to deal with him later. It's not like he's going to the police. Now drive." He turned to Josie and pointed his gun close to her face.

"Where are we going?"

"You'll see."

"Well, I need to know where I'm going if you want me to drive there." She snapped. Michael cringed, expecting Samuel to explode in a rage, but he couldn't help but get some satisfaction from her talking to him like that.

"Straight ahead." He waved his gun, gesturing for her to go forward.

Josie pulled away from the roadside and started driving. The car jolted a couple of times as she stalled, trying to get used to the unfamiliar vehicle.

"Woman drivers, am I right?" Samuel joked, but his face was dead-pan. "Slow down when I tell you."

With it being so late and being in the middle of nowhere, they did not pass another car for the short journey. Samuel asked Josie to start slowing down until they reached a tiny gap in the trees at the side of the road and he asked her to pull over.

Chapter Thirty Two

They entered the small path in-between the trees which had barely been visible from the roadside—Samuel must have known what he was looking for. Branches scratched their bare arms as they progressed through the undergrowth. A sudden light barely illuminated the narrow path as Samuel lit a small torch that he must have had stashed in his pocket. . It was a small trail that looked like it had been forged with a machete, and it only got denser as they made their way through as ferns curled around their legs and tree roots snagged their feet as they walked.

It wasn't long until they reached a clearing. Now it was only this one man against the two of them. Sure he had a gun, but if Michael struck when he least expected it, surely it wouldn't take much to catch him guard. Samuel was distracted as he scanned the jungle with his torch, until the weak beam revealed a large black hole in the ground—an open mouth feeding on the vegetation that surrounded it, swallowing it whole. Michael had no interest in finding out what was inside there, but as Samuel shined his torchlight, some strange little voice in the back of his head dared him to. That little voice that wondered what it would be like to jump when stood on a tall building.

"Do you know what a cenote is?" Samuel asked, shining the torch in Michael's face. He squinted and looked down at the forest floor, not answering. He remembered the first cenote he had visited in Mexico. It was huge, much bigger than this one. The water inside was crystal clear and connected to a network of underground caves. Tourists gathered at the opening, looking in, plucking up the courage to make the drop into the blue water below, and when they did, everybody would cheer. This was different.

"You know there are over 6,000 cenotes in this area alone, and that doesn't include the undiscovered ones." Samuel got close to Michael, trying to force him back towards the opening. Michael took a step back, not being able to stand being so close. "You know the Mayans believed that Cenotes were gateways to the underworld?" Samuel said, his face glowing underneath from the torch in his left hand. His gun was in his right hand, lowered, so that the gun was pointing somewhere around Michael's thigh. Samuel got closer. "You know what else?"

"What?" Michael asked. He opened his hand that had been clenched into a fist at his side, and wondered if he grabbed at the gun now, would he be able to move it away quickly enough to avoid getting shot? He could twist Samuel's hand in the other direction. Maybe he would misfire into the forest. Maybe he could then catch him off balance. Knock him into the hole in the ground. Too many maybes, but then again, he had nothing to lose.

"The Mayans would also drop their sacrifices into the cenotes. Pots, jugs, precious stones, food, cloth… people. It's so important to keep tradition alive. Don't you think?"

Michael reacted on instinct, his hand working independently of his brain, reaching for the gun. He heard the sound before he felt the pain. So loud in the deathly quiet night. Ringing though the trees, waking up whatever animals had been quiet until now. The solid ground beneath his feet gave way as he stumbled backwards, falling from the precipice, and in seconds his body slammed against the water like a stinging-slap.

The shock of the cold water made him gasp, but as his head went underneath the surface, he couldn't breathe. He sank from the momentum of the drop, sliding deeper and deeper, to a whole new level of blackness. For a brief moment, we wondered what it would be like to drown. He moved his arms in a swimming motion, but could not tell which direction he needed to go until his body naturally started floating towards the surface. As he broke through to the world above, he sucked in all the air he could and panted as he tried to stay afloat. The disturbed water lapped against the limestone walls.

Now his head was above water, and even though he could barely see, he could tell how huge the cave was from the inside by the way the sounds echoed off of the walls. It had the acoustics of being in a stone cathedral. It had to have been much bigger than it looked from the outside, because he swam for a while before his hands made contact with the cold, damp stone that made up the sides of the cave.

The water got shallower towards the edge and he could stand up. He leaned against the stone, resting his weight against it as he waited for his breathing to catch up with him. Now he didn't have to worry about staying afloat, the pain made itself known again. He touched the side of his torso and winced as his fingers touched the exposed flesh through the rip in his t-shirt. He must have been hit when he tried to grab the gun. The bullet appeared to have grazed his side. He couldn't let the pain overwhelm him and tried to distract himself, and wondered what the hell he was going to do now.

He looked up but couldn't see anything. It was mostly black, except for the odd flash of white as water rippled and the tiniest amount of light glistened off of the damp walls. He couldn't see the mouth of the cave.

Fragments of limestone exploded near his head, and reverberations echoed off of the cave-walls as a shot rained down from above. The water exploded near his feet, liquid shooting up into the air like a volcanic eruption. Michael dodged, hopping around clumsily like he was walking on hot-coals. He waited, chest heaving, as he flattened his body against the wall, but no more shots came.

The voice from above was an incoherent mumbling from where Michael stood. He desperately tried to make out the words, to have some kind of clue as to what was going on up there. Another shot fired out, but it wasn't fired into the cenote, not that he could tell anyway. A sinking feeling lurched inside of him, like going over a bump in the road. His heart sunk. It had to be Josie, surely. Another shot fired. It sounded quieter this time, further away maybe. He hoped Josie was making a run for it. Maybe she could outrun him. There were plenty of hiding places in the thick jungle. There was a chance, and he held onto that sliver of hope as tightly as he could.

There had to be a way out of this pit. As his eyes adjusted

somewhat to this new level of darkness he could make out cave walls curved over him. Not going straight up, but creating a dome above. The opening was tiny in comparison. There was no way he was climbing out of there, not unless he could dangle from the ceiling of the cave. He had felt vines or dangling algae brush past him when he had fallen in, but there was nothing that dangled down far enough for him to climb up it.

The walls were impossible slippery and his injured finger made it almost impossible to get any kind of purchase on the stone. All he could do was try and think, to push through the fog that closed in around his brain. The only thing he could hear now was the occasional drop of water. Nothing was going on above him. He started walking along the wall, feeling for any craggy areas, or a drier section of rock that he could use to elevate himself.

As he made his way around towards the other side of the cave, feeling with his hands, the dank, musty smell of the cave got stronger, until it smelled strongly like rotting leaves, no not that, something else. He shuffled further, and further. He recognized the smell now. It reminded him of when he had found a dead raccoon under the front steps of the house. It was the height of summer and he would never forget the smell as he had to scrape its stiff corpse into a garbage bag.

He stopped immediately and hurried back the way he came, telling himself some jungle animal had just fallen in. Not one of Samuel's victims. He didn't want to imagine the look of the bodies while he sat trapped in the dark. If he was never found, he could be stuck here a long time with them. It would get light soon, and then he would be forced to confront whatever was there. He got as far away as he could from the source of the rancid odor but he could still smell it, like his brain wouldn't let forget. He imagined what a corpse might look like if it had been submerged in water for days. His mind conjured flashes of purple, swollen flesh, bulging eyes. Flesh falling away. Slippage. It was only now he wished he had spent less time looking at gory sites in the darkest corners of the World Wide Web.

He tried to think about something else, but started wondering how long hypothermia might take to set in. Although it was warm in the jungle, the cold stone and damp atmosphere had raised goosebumps across his bare arms and his hairs stood to attention. There was only so long he could stand it. His feet were already numb. Now he'd had time to process what had happened, he fought the urge to sob. This wasn't how he was supposed to go out. Cold. Uncomfortable. In pain. Terrified. If Samuel had killed Josie, this would all have been for nothing. Just piling misery on misery. The sorrow branched out from Tanya, to her parents, to Josie. It then crept from Josie, to Miguel, Miguel's family, to himself, maybe even to Aleksander. One tragedy had ruined so many lives. Although everything had turned to shit, Michael wasn't sure he still wouldn't have joined Josie if he could go back in time. He envisioned an alternate universe in which everyone was still alive. Fantasizing was the only thing that could get him from one minute to the next, not just in this dark place, but through his entire life.

He went to wrap him arms around himself to keep warm but cried out in pain as he touched the gash and just held his arms limply to his side. His broken finger throbbed and the wound on his side started to itch as he imagined the water he had been sharing with a decaying body lapping over it. He screamed. First he screamed curse words into the void at the top of his lungs, and then he called for help. This then devolved into guttural animal-like sounds.

Once he had exhausted himself he leaned his forehead against the solid rock and let silent tears fall. Even if Josie wasn't dead, a worse fate could be befalling her right now. As he thought about all the awful things that could have been happening to her at that exact moment, light flooded in from above.

"Michael." The voice called, distorted by the curves of the

walls, but it definitely wasn't Samuel.

"Help." He called back hoarsely.

"They took my car."

"Miguel. Is that you?" Michael's cries turned to hysterical laughter.

"Yes. Hold on." Miguel's voice echoed back.

The crushing feeling of dread subsided somewhat, but he still had no idea how he was going to get back up. Samuel had probably left him there, assuming he was as good as dead. Maybe Samuel had underestimated him.

The beam lit up the stalactites that hung down like icicles. "Okay. Listen. There used to be a ladder, but no more. You need to swim. There is smaller cenote connected by the underground cavern. I used to do when I was young. I did it with no gear. I left a safety wire. It will maybe still be there. You follow it all the way to other side. You feel for it. It is at the deeper end. Go right."

The things Miguel was saying were impossible and Michael wondered if he was really expecting him to do this. To dive into pitch blackness without a source of oxygen. He must have gone mad. The only thing that made him go through with it, was what had happened to Miguel. He felt responsible to, and if Miguel had to endure seeing his wife like he did, hanging from the balcony, then Michael would have to suck it up and endure this. The thought of it made his blood run colder than it already was. There was no way he could do this. He struggled to hold his breath for long period of time. He hated it, that feeling. The water splashed around him as he waded towards the other end of the pool. Water came up higher and he shuddered with the cold as it got to his waist. Miguel did his best to keep the light in the right place.

"You're going to have to go under now." Miguel called.

What am I doing here? Michael mumbled a quiet prayer to a god he didn't believe in before dunking his head under. The shock of the water overtook him completely and he brought his head back up. He wasn't ready for this—to suffocate to death. The pain would end at some point, no matter what happened. He sucked in the biggest lung-full of air he could muster and submerged his head again. Plunging himself down with urgency he groped around for this rope Miguel spoke of. If Miguel had managed it once, he could too. Rock, rock, more rock, and something thin and coarse. Yes. He clutched the wire and fought against his own buoyancy until there was only rock above him. He pulled hard on the rope to bring himself down and stop his head scraping along the stone above and his ears popped. Worried about pulling the secured line from the cavern floor he instead, opted to use his hand to keep his head protected from the jaggedness of the surface.

It was a tight space but he tried not to think about that, which lasted all of five seconds until he thought about what might happen if he got stuck. Bubbles came out of his mouth as the tiny bit of air left in it escaped. It wouldn't be much longer until his brain would demand that he open his mouth. He had already lasted longer than he ever thought possible. His lungs started to burn as he wondered how much further could it be? The panic took over and he started scrabbling wildly and lost his grip on the safety wire.

Chapter Thirty Three

Michael propelled himself forward, kicking and grabbing onto bits of stone and pulling himself. The wound on his arm burning red hot, the only part of him that was warm.

At the point where he knew he had a few seconds left, without even trying, he started to drift upwards. There was nothing above him anymore and he rose upwards. He tried to propel himself faster by kicking his feet but it felt like an eternity. That moment when the water broke above him he was overjoyed. If he wasn't so busy gasping he would have been crying. All the fear that had built up inside of him escaped with his ragged breaths, but his elation was short lived when he realized he still had to get out of there.

Even though he struggled to see he got the sense this cavern was smaller than the last. The noises he made did not travel so far before they bounced back to him. He made his way to the nearest wall. This cenote did not have a shallow part for him to escape the water and he stayed afloat, barely.

When the light from Miguel's torch shone into the hole, he breathed a sigh of relief. Although this cenote was much smaller the hole was bigger and it looked like it might be possible to climb up, although he couldn't imagine doing that in his state. The light revealed the nooks and crannies. His desire to be out of the water overtook his fatigue and he swam to the nearest section of wall he could find while Miguel illuminated the way.

He managed to wedge his foot into a crack and put his weight on it while feeling around for anything he could grab onto. It was still slick, but not as slippery as the last time he tried. The lack of plant-matter attached to it helped. He had only tried rock-climbing once in an indoor place with specially designed hand grips, security harnesses and padded floors. One slip of the hand would be all it took. He may just fall back into the water, or he could end up impaled on a stalagmite.

The thought of making progress, only to have to start again filled him with a heavy feeling of dread in his stomach. He wouldn't let it happen and forced himself to concentrate more than he ever had before. Not acting too quickly. His core muscles tensed as he tried to keep his balance when climbing and heaved himself up to the next overhanging piece of rock. The tension made a tearing sensation in his side and he was certain he could feel warm blood gush from his injury. He ignored it and forged on, his biceps trembling as he hung on as tight as he could. The closer he got to the top, the more he rushed. He just wanted to be at the top already so he could spread out on the floor and let himself go for a second.

When he got about two-thirds up, he reached the roots that hung down. He was going to have to grab onto them, but had no idea if they would hold his weight—there was no other way around it. His hand gripped onto the rough root and tugged. It seemed secure enough. He avoided using his pinkie finger entirely as if any pressure was placed on it, a stabbing pain made him want to let go. He moved one of his feet higher up, balancing on a small piece of something. As his other hand reached for another root, whatever was keeping his foot in place broke away and his body weight tried to pull him down and he jolted, tightly gripping the root with both hands. The yanking motion sent pain shooting across his various injuries like lightning bolts and he swung gently from side to side, waiting for the pain to subside before finding another foot-hold. After taking a few seconds to recover from the shock of it all, it was time for the last push. He ignored the burning sensation of friction as the roots dug into his hands. He was never one for pep-talks, but this time was the exception. *You can do this. You got this.* Using every last bit of body strength he had, he climbed the hanging tree-root like a rope. He remembered having to climb a rope when he was at school, and for some reason his physical education teacher insisted all the other kids watch. His upper body strength wasn't much then, and it probably wasn't much now, but adrenaline was a surprising thing, making the impossible, possible. If the circumstances were right, your body could put up with all sorts of punishment. He was so close now. Miguel's face waited above him. When he got close enough to reach him Miguel held out an arm and he took it gladly. Even with Miguel helping, that last push over the lip of the opening, felt like conquering Everest.

Once he rolled onto the flat earth of the forest Michael laughed. Compared to the harsh rock, the ferns beneath him felt like a soft mattress. Every muscle shook, partly from cold, partly from exhaustion. He smiled as he saw stars through gaps in the trees.

"You look like shit."

"I've been better." It was only now, when letting go, that Michael realized just how weak he felt. Just a moment ago he had been climbing, but now, he couldn't even imagine standing up.

"You need to see someone." Miguel looked him over. The concern in Miguel's face didn't inspire confidence.

"Who?"

"Someone needs to stitch you up."

"It's fine. I just need a little rest." He closed his eyes. This was a fine place to sleep, enveloped by ferns, watching the stars above.

"They took my car. Need to call someone, but I can't. Most of my guys were Samuel's guys too."

"There is this one guy," said Michael.

Chapter Thirty Four

They waited by the roadside for ten minutes before one of them spoke. "So this friend of yours, you trust him?" Miguel asked

"Implicitly?" Michael had perked up a little now, but staying upright was a struggle, so he sat on the gravel. He had used Miguel's phone to call Alex to pick them up. Hearing his voice and knowing he was okay was something at least.

Miguel unbuttoned his shirt, took it off and slipped his t-shirt over his head, before putting his other shirt back on. "Here, take this. Use it to stop bleeding. Put pressure on it."

"Thanks." Michael bunched up the T-shirt and pressed it against his side, although it looked like most of the blood had congealed now.

"No tighter. You have to put real pressure on it."

The headlights of an oncoming car temporarily blinded the pair of them. Michael wouldn't have been surprised if it had been Samuel, coming to finish the job, but he recognized the car as Alex's as it got closer. The car pulled in front of them, coming to a sudden stop.

As his muscles had grown stiff, Michael lowered himself slowly onto the front passenger's seat, and Aleksander's eyes widened when he saw the state he was in.

"I'm so sorry, man. I didn't know what to do. I should have come back. Where is Josie?"

"Thank you for coming. I don't know where she is. I think Samuel still has her. This is Miguel by the way."

Miguel let himself in the back and thanked Alex for picking them up.

"So what now? Do we take you to a hospital?" He asked Michael.

Miguel spoke before Michael could even open his mouth. "No! No hospital. We get a sewing kit. I do it."

"Where are we going to find a sewing kit?" Michael broke into a cold sweat, thinking of an amateur sewing him up with some cotton and thread. His mind tried to conjure up any way around it. "There is this one guy." It seemed like a distant memory now, before things had gotten out of hand. That man he had met briefly in the bar in Arelanes was a surgeon. He didn't know if he could trust the guy but he wanted a professional working on him. "There was this guy I met. He was a doctor, a surgeon. I met him in Arelanes"

"Álvaro?" Miguel asked wondering why Miguel hadn't suggested it if he knew the guy.

"You know him?"

"He'd always be in La Cocina De Maya. Liked the ladies."

"Yes. That restaurant. Is he a good guy? He gave me the creeps a bit but I feel like he's harmless enough."

"I know him only a little. He's not in the game. Why would he help you?"

"Maybe if I pay him?" Michael wasn't sure what surgeons earned in this area, and if he had anything of value to offer the almost perfect stranger.

"How would we even get in touch with this man?"

"He gave me his number. All my contacts are available in the cloud. It's worth a try?"

"Not to be a downer, but what's the plan beyond that?" Alex chimed in.

"We get Josie." Michael didn't even know where to begin, but he could worry about that later.

Aleksander's satellite navigation struggled to find Álvaro's house, but eventually they found it nestled in a town close to Arelanes. The place was less built up and more rustic. The simple houses nestled in amongst trees. Many looked hand-built by the owners with mismatched bricks and scrap iron roofs. The house they were looking for was the only blue house on that street, and they pulled up outside onto the dusty driveway.

Álvaro had been awake when they called, on his way back from work after a long shift, the annoyance and exhaustion clearly apparent over loud-speaker. He let Miguel do most of the talking, and here they were. They walked up to the boxy house with a satellite dish poking out of the top, and Miguel knocked on the door. They heard the noise of someone moving stuff around in the house, and Álvaro opened the door, gingerly peeking his head out to find three people waiting for him on the other side. His face looked so different from the other day, and his hair disheveled, dark shadows under his eyes.

"You better come in," he said in hushed tones.

Álvaro already had some stuff ready: a bowl of water, towels, alcohol, cotton, and some instruments that he may have taken from work. Michael hoped he wouldn't get in trouble on his behalf. A long wooden table had been cleared and placed in the middle of the room. He assumed Álvaro expected him to lie on it.

"Shit, they weren't lying." He inspected the more obvious gash on Michael's arm first before switching his attention to his torso. "Do you have the money?"

"I don't have anything. My wallet is—"

Miguel and Aleksander both pulled cash from their wallets and handed it over to Álvaro, who stuck it in his back pocket. "Shall we get started then?"

The table didn't look particularly sturdy and Michael hesitated before putting his whole weight on it, but it did the job.

"Okay. First, I will clean."

Michael looked up at the gray ceiling and was more comfortable than he had anticipated.

"Ahhh. Shit. You could have warned me" The stinging pain made him unable to control his words as Álvaro poured alcohol over the wound on his arm.

"I find it's easier if you don't expect it."

"Hmm. I'm not convinced." Michael braced himself this time and managed to stay almost silent as Álvaro disinfected the injury on his side. He hadn't even brought himself to look at it. It was best left a mystery to him.

He glanced over at the instruments that lay on a metal tray and decided he should just keep his eyes glued to the ceiling. He wished he could have had a stiff drink before the next stage, but Álvaro said it wouldn't be a good idea. Maybe he wanted him to feel as much pain as possible, to punish him from keeping him from sleep. *Mind over matter. It's just mind over matter.* It definitely hurt, he couldn't lie about that. It was just about manageable. Alex walked over to the other side of the table and looked down at him. "You're brave man." Concentrating on Alex's face and words distracted him from the pain a little. It was a strange sensation, sometimes sharp pain, but others just a weird pinching feeling. After not too long, Álvaro had finished with his arm and offered Michael to have a break after wrapping it up in some dressing to protect it.

Before starting again, Álvaro forced Michael to eat something and gave him some strong antibiotics. The powdery pills got stuck in his dry throat as he swallowed and disintegrated, leaving a harsh, bitter taste that reminded him of the Pentobarbital.

"So. You should put a good word in for me with Josie."

"I will." Michael hadn't told Álvaro the details of what had happened and had kept Josie out of it up until this point.

"Okay. Ready to carry on?"

"As ready as I'll ever be." He steeled himself for the next onslaught of pain. After a minute of grimacing and gritting his teeth, he started to get used to it, like when he got his one and only tattoo, he hadn't got used to it enough to end up having another. The tugging and pinching at his side was somehow less painful than the arm, and it was comforting to know it was almost over. He looked over at Miguel, who was sat on a wooden chair and stared down at the floor. His face was devoid of emotion at that point, nothing behind his eyes.

"There you are." Álvaro took a square shaped piece of dressing and secured it onto Michael's side with surgical tape.

Michael breathed a sigh of relief before slowly bringing his legs down over the side of the table. "Would you mind checking this out?" He held up his hand to Álvaro showing his bent finger.

"Ouch. They really did a number on you. Note sure I really have what I need to sort that out." He thought for a moment and then disappeared into another room for a minute and came back eating an ice-cream.

"Does ice-cream help you think?" Alex asked. Álvaro wolfed down the ice cream in a few mouthfuls and disinfected the wooden ice-cream stick. He held it up to Michael's fingers and used it as a splint, keeping the pinkie finger joined with the ring finger as he wrapped a bandage around it.

"This will have to do for now. Now I mean this in the nicest possible way. Please get out of my house."

Chapter Thirty Five

Back on the road again, Aleksander asked that inevitable question. "What are we going to do now?"

"We shoul—"

Miguel interrupted Michael. "I am going to deal with Samuel."

"And what will you do when you find him?" Michael asked.

"Wrap my hands around his miserable neck." The empty look he'd had earlier changed. His jaw clenched and his hands were balled into fists as if he was ready to swing a punch at the next person who spoke. The quiet tension on the car was palpable, and then a phone rang, some annoyingly upbeat ring-tone.

Miguel unclenched his hand and picked it up. "Hello," he said gruffly. "How did you get this number?" The disgust oozed from his voice. Michael knew it was Samuel straight away by the hatred in Miguel's face. He couldn't imagine him loathing anyone else that strongly. Eventually Miguel spoke again. "We will be there." He spat, and hung up.

"What did he say? Is Josie alive?" Michael searched Miguel's eyes for a reaction.

"He wants me, you and Alex to come to El Verdugo. It has to be all of us. And it has to be alone."

"The hell we're going in there alone. God knows how many people he has waiting for us."

"No Policia. That will guarantee their death."

"Not this time. If we do this how they want, we all die. If we have backup, at least some of us make it out alive. You're the only one of us that's armed. I'm telling you, going in there alone if a stupid idea." Michael couldn't believe he was talking to him this way. Despite having a soft spot for the man for saving his life, there was something about him he still found intimidating.

"Okay. We go in first. Have a head start. We can call the police just before. Then they think we're alone."

Aleksander stopped the car in the middle of the road. "Listen guys. I'm sorry but, I can't do this. This is too much. I don't want to die, man."

"It needs to be all of us," said Miguel.

Michael could see the agitation rising in his face. "Come on, Miguel. I met Alex randomly in some hostel. He owes me nothing. He has already done so much for me. I can't ask him to die for us. He has no reason to die for us. You know it's not fair to ask that of him."

"You want to talk fair?" His loud voice made Michael tense up.

"Fine, fine. I go." Alex tried to placate him.

"Alex. Your being stupid. If Miguel scares you, Samuel Hernandez and someone nicknamed the fucking Executioner is going to make you have a fucking heart-attack. This is life and death we're talking here. Miguel is not going to shoot you. Trust me. Don't be pressured into doing something you might regret."

"You have no idea what I am capable of." Miguel got out of the car to take a breath and leaned against the wheel arch, rubbing his face. Michael opened his door and walked around to check on him. Miguel looked thoughtful for a minute before speaking again. "That cenote. I used to play there when I was a kid, and a teenager. You know what I use it for now?"

"What?"

"Samuel and I have dumped bodies there. I put bodies in there." Miguel was crying now, and it shocked Michael to his core. Certain people just were not supposed to cry. "I've killed. Not because the person was any worse than I, just because they were on the wrong side. I need to make things right."

Michael leaned next to him, taking in a deep breath of fresh air. "You know, forcing an innocent guy to take a bullet, it's not right."

"I know." Miguel sighed and went to get back in the car, still looking pissed-off.

***

The sun was rising by the time they started making their way to the address that Samuel had given. The fiery orange-streaked canvas did not inspire Michael the way the sunset had. It glowed like a warning light, flashing just for them. As far as Miguel believed, El Verdugo's main property was on the outskirts of Playa del Carmen, and he had never been to this place before. Located between Chetumal and Felipe Carrillo Puerto, there were no other properties on this stretch of road, just trees, road, trees, road, and more trees. They would have driven straight past the place if Miguel hadn't noticed it, nestled in the jungle, hidden from the main road. He shouted for Aleksander to apply the brakes. Not wanting to be too close, Alex carried on, until they were, what he felt was a safe distance away. He parked up the car and shut off the engine.

"So, here we are." He had that look, that slightly awkward look that travelers had before going their separate ways, one of sadness and sentimentality, nostalgia for a period of time that wasn't even quite over yet. "I hope you understand—"

"Say no more." Michael could tell Alex felt bad. He could tell by the guilty look on his face. His head hanging down, not quite able to look him in the eye, like a dog who had stolen food from the table. People didn't sacrifice themselves for people they barely knew, that was a given. Hell, a lot of people barely make sacrifices for people they have known for years: colleagues, lovers, family.

"We will have a drink when this is all over. I think we should have reunion a year from now. What'ya say?"

Michael knew this was an impossibility on so many levels, but if it made Alex feel better. "Sure." He patted his shoulder in a brotherly fashion.

"Will you reconsider waiting for the police? No need to make more dangerous than need be."

"The plan's the same. You call them before you leave. Then you get as far away from here as possible. And no matter what happens, always remember that game of ring of fire in Pueblo."

"How could I forget? You drink enough to bring down a horse." They went for a formal handshake. It was the only way Michael could think of to display his mutual respect. Michael got out of the car and inhaled the fresh morning air. All Miguel gave Alex was a nod before getting out of the car and checking his weapon.

"Let's do this then." Michael announced. They walked back in the direction of the house and he took one last look back at the car, feeling the 6 am breeze skim his arms and face. Everything felt heightened—the slightest sound accentuated. Shoes scuffing on dirt. The gentle murmurs of the forest. He could still barely wrap his head around the concept that once one was dead, they could feel nothing. The harder he tried to imagine the absence of anything, the more he struggled. Consciousness is all he had known, and soon, every last piece of himself, besides the physical vessel, would be gone. He always rationalized that a person was really just a bunch of synapses firing, nothing special. Memories meant nothing at the end. Everyone was the same. Flesh and blood. A bundle of impulses, urges and instinct. Biological computers processing our surroundings just like everyone else. There were billions of people on this earth. On this sunny Tuesday with clear skies, his imminent death meant little in the grand scheme of things. The world would keep spinning. His mind always spouted this kind of gibberish when he thought he was close to the end. He needed to snap out of it, be on guard, present.

The house was not far now. "So, we still just walking through the front door?" Michael asked. He was essentially just a human sacrifice at this point, someone to throw into the cenote, an offering for better things to come. It was unlikely his sacrifice would mean anything. It wasn't as if Josie was getting out of there either. He was just voluntarily adding himself to the body count. At least this way, he might be remembered as a hero by someone out there, rather than a coward, not that he believed that suicide made someone a coward anyway, but it was hard not to internalize the comments he had seen on the internet whenever the latest celebrity suicide would hit social media. Death was death. Humanity liked to pretend that offering yourself to death was noble when it was in society's best interest. Being cannon fodder was okay, but there was no need to lose a willing wage-slave if they didn't have to.

"Michael! Head in the game." Miguel's stern voice made him stand to attention. "Take this." He passed him a blade. It wasn't much, and they would probably be searched and disarmed upon entering.

"I wonder how many men they have?" It was all starting to feel startlingly real now. It was strangely quiet, and they couldn't see anyone from the front of the building. The place looked abandoned, with no lights on and off-white bars over the dark windows.

The surrounding forest had taken over the boundary walls. Vines crept their way up, weaving through gaps in the brick, pushing out chunks of mortar as they consumed the wall.

Chapter Thirty Six

It felt strange watching Miguel just go up to the door and knock, like a guest coming around for drinks. Nothing happened. The door remained closed. Miguel pounded his fist on the door this time.

"This doesn't feel right." Michael said, stating the obvious.

"Maybe we go around the back." Miguel suggested, peering down the overgrown path down the side of the house, and at that moment the sound of a security latch sent him racing to the front of the door. The minute the latch had been lifted, before the door could be opened more than half an inch, his foot smashed against the door and he burst into the house like a charging bull, gun in hand. The door had hurtled forward with such force that it slammed back on itself after it hit the wall, almost shutting in Michael's face, and as he went to open it the ear-splitting noise of Miguel's gun firing sent him ducking for cover. The door creaked open, and he waited, crouched, with his hands over his head, to see what it revealed. A man Michael didn't recognize lay on the floor. The mouth hung open so wide, it looked like it was disconnected from the jaw. Blood covered the floor and wall, the splatter marks almost reaching up to the ceiling. Samuel stood against the back wall with another man, watching as two men restrained Miguel, holding him down on the floor. He spat and shouted as he struggled. Even between the two of them, they could barely keep him down. The rage wouldn't let him stop. Michael was surprised they hadn't killed him already and wondered what they wanted from them. They could have been killed a million times over already. He stepped inside, lifting his legs up high to avoid treading on the body in front of him. He felt strangely accustomed to seeing dead bodies now.

The man that stood with Samuel stepped out from behind the shadows at the back of the room and walked towards Michael. Each step, slow and deliberate. His footsteps echoed on the hard-bare floor "It's nice to finally meet you. I see your friend isn't here, but no worry. It wasn't hard to find out all about Aleksander Janssen. He will be dealt with." The man was short and slim. Although he hadn't introduced himself yet, Michael was certain this was El Verdugo. The way Samuel carried himself around this man. He respectfully kept back, hands down in front of him, not saying a word, like a mourner at a funeral. Somehow Michael had expected something different of El Verdugo, not this compact man that stood at his eye level. The news that Aleksander would not come out of this unscathed should have been the last straw, but he felt compelled not to let his emotions show.

"Where is Josie?" He managed to get the words out without stuttering or wavering.

The man nodded at Samuel, who made himself scarce. "She's coming. You can call me Antonio, not that stupid nickname people insist on calling me." He ran his fingers through his wild, curly hair. Michael wondered if he'd made his hair so tall to compensate for his height.

One of the men held Miguel down as the other man kicked him in the side repeatedly. Miguel rolled over onto his back groaning and the man stomped his foot into his gut at full force, and again, and again. The sound so visceral, Michael could feel it vicariously in his own stomach and put his hand in front of it, as if to protect it as he wondered what pain he would have to endure.

Josie stumbled in as Samuel dragged her by her arm that was tied behind her back. A deep blue and purple bruise took up most of the upper right hand-side of her face. They stared into each other's eyes as if trying to connect on some greater level until Samuel pushed her down onto a chair by her shoulder. Even with the bruising, it was obvious she had been crying from her damp red face and swollen eyes.

"Why haven't you killed us already?" He had avoided asking this question up until now, as he hadn't been ready for the answer.

"I wanted everyone here for the surprise." Antonio said casually, as if he was referring to a birthday cake.

"What surprise? Enough with the fucking games already." He couldn't believe he was saying this, to this man of all people. Michael had never been able to stand up for himself, and now it was the worst time to do so, but he couldn't control the words from tumbling out of his mouth.

"The surprise isn't here yet. Take a seat." He pulled out a chair from a table on the other side of the room, and the chair legs scraped along the floor as he dragged it along and placing it next to Josie. Before he could sit down, Samuel patted him down, running his hands up and down his legs and sides.

"When will you learn?" He took the retractable knife from Michael's pocket and thrust him down onto the hard chair, sending a twinge up his spine.

Michael turned to Josie. "I'm so glad you're alive. What did they do to you?" The look in her eyes made the sting of tears well up behind his. "Sorry we took so long."

"Don't you dare be sorry." Her tears picked up, trickling down like raindrops down a window. "I thought you were dead. The gun. The cenote. I know I've been awful. I'm so sorry."

"Well, now you know the truth, there's no need to feel guilty because of me. You did me a favor, Josie. At least my death will mean something now."

"But it won't. It will be for nothing. All of us. You. Me. Miguel. Aleksander. You warned me. You warned me, but I didn't listen. I just couldn't let it go. It's all I thought about for over a year. It's one of the things Tanya always had a go at me for. She'd always tell me to chill out. Just let whatever shall be… be. Maybe I should have listened to her, been more like her."

Vibrations went off in Antonio's pocket and he pulled his phone out, eagerly pushing the answer button as he lifted the phone to his ear and spoke in Spanish to the person at the other end of the phone. Once his conversation was finished, he gave Samuel a knowing nod. "It's time. Don't you go anywhere." He flashed them his teeth before rushing to the front of the house, skipping over the corpse that lay in front of the door, being careful not to stand in the pool of blood that had accumulated beneath, and slipped out of the door.

"Any last words?" Josie asked, not taking her eyes away

from the front door.

"I don't know if there's anything left to say." He lied. The problem was there were too many things to say, yet no matter how bad things got, how vulnerable he was, he could never bring himself to say them.

The two men tied Miguel up, wrapping copious amounts of rope around his arms and feet. His belly was pressed against the floor, and despite one of them having a gun to his head, he resisted with every fiber of his being, his face contorted with the effort as he shuffled across the ground. They left him to squirm as they went to attend to the body. Each of them took a side and started shuffling the body across the room into a dark corner. They hadn't bothered lifting the body fully, and the arched back dragged in the darkening blood, a crimson smear soaking into the concrete. After chucking a burlap covering over the body, they walked over to front of the sparse room and stood on each side of the front door, waiting, facing each other with their guns ready, down at a slight angle. The covering did little to conceal the body when there was such a prominent blood trail towards it.

The door opened, slowly, like the curtain unveiling a play that was about to start. The sliver of light grew bigger with dust particles dancing in its ray. He could only see their outlines at first as the sun shone from behind them, but once they stepped into the room, and Samuel's head blocked out the bulk of the sun, he could make out the three figures stood there a little better. Samuel and Antonio on each side, but following slightly behind. The figure in the middle in mid conversation, stopped just after their feet went over the threshold, and as they turned, they noticed the armed man waiting for them on the other side of the door. "What's going on, Antonio? This doesn't look like it would make a good hotel. I mean, there's no amenities nearby for a start. If it's another lab you want to start, you should have said—" The voice stopped, and the person stepped away from the light, scanning the room as they blinked repeatedly. The men at the door closed in on her. The face. That angular chin. Those wide eyes. Black shiny hair falling poker straight at her shoulders. If it wasn't for the blunt fringe, revealing outfit and telltale lines around the around her eyes, he would have sworn it was Josie.

Chapter Thirty Seven

Her hand fell away from her hip and hung limply at her side. With a look of shock as if she had been slapped, the color drained from her face, going from red to white in a heartbeat. "Antonio?" She turned to him as if looking for some sort of explanation and grabbed his hands, holding them in hers. "What's going on?" Her head turned as the two men positioned themselves in front of the door, then turned back to him. "Antonio?"

Michael tore his eyes away from the doppelganger in front of him and looked at Josie, still as a statue, and pale as one too. It looked as if every last drop of blood had been drained from her body.

The woman walked across the room towards where he and Josie sat. Her heels stabbing the floor with each step. He had assumed that she had seen them before, but it was only as she got closer, that a look of recognition filled her eyes. Her lips moved as if she was going to speak, but only a stunted noise came out, barely making its way past her throat. Neither Josie nor the woman moved from their respective positions, they just looked at each other.

"Tanya." The word came from Josie's mouth, but it didn't sound like one sister addressing another. Her lips struggled to form the name, as if her mouth was getting used to it for the first time. Antonio came up behind Tanya, his lips close to her ear. "I think you need to sit down." He looked down at the chair that he had pulled out for her.

She just stood there, blinking, confused. "I don't—"

"Someone came looking for you." He glanced at Josie.

"What happened to her?" she asked shakily.

Michael couldn't understand why she wasn't addressing her sister directly and looking to Antonio for answers, but he couldn't bring himself to react beyond a stunned silence.

"You weren't supposed to come." Tanya looked down at the floor rather than in Josie's eyes.

"Tanya. You should really be sitting down for this." Antonio grabbed her shoulders and forced her down on the chair. She looked up at him, eyes wide and pleading. "I didn't know she would come." She said, her hands reached out for his, but he instead, unholstered his weapon, and started polishing it with a corner of his shirt. "Come on. We knew this was never going to last. It always had an expiry date." He took a dramatic step back from her, as if dissociating from her completely.

"But you left your wife for me. You said I was—"

"Jesus. People say things. We had some fun. You've been useful, and now you're a liability."

Tanya went to stand, but he impeded her momentum with a firm hand to the shoulder. "Don't make this awkward, Tanya. No-one likes a woman who can't take a hint. It's over."

"What are you doing?" She lurched forward, trying to snatch the weapon from his hand, but he grabbed her by the hair, pulling her head towards him, and digging the muzzle of his handgun into her forehead. Tanya started wailing. "You lied to me," she screamed dramatically like the lead of a tele novella. She lifted her head up. Tears had already started making their way down her face. Following the curves of her cheeks and clinging to her chin for a moment before dripping down.

"But… the things we did… I love you. You weren't faking it, I know you weren't," she shouted, red-faced.

Michael jumped in his chair when Josie sprung forward, propelling herself at his sister like a wrecking ball. Her chair crashed down behind her, and she launched Tanya off of hers, slamming her against the hard concrete floor.

"You fucking idiot. What the fuck did you do?." She sat on top of her and slapped her across the face. Her hand connecting with her sister's cheek like a crack of thunder. The sound echoing around the room. Even witnessing the ferocity of it made Michael flinch and want to rub the side of his face to sooth the imagined pain. Tanya tried to push her sister off, but she slapped her again. And again. Each slap slightly lighter than the last as if the rage was dissipating with each strike. Samuel, Antonio, and their two sicarios watched on with a thinly concealed look of amusement.

From the corner of his eye, Michael could see Miguel had somehow managed to untie his arms and was yanking at the rope around his feet. If there was a time to act, it had to be now. If the police were coming though, was it worth holding back, biding time? Samuel and Antonio did not seem in any particular hurry. Maybe they knew something he didn't. The two hit men were the closest now, they even had their backs turned, transfixed with the scuffle taking place on the floor.

Throwing logic out of the window, he dived for one of the men's guns. He had it. It was heavy in his hand. He had no idea how to use it. The man whose gun he had snatched had barely noticed, and Michael grabbed the man in front of him as the other unnamed man aimed and pulled his trigger. The force of the bullet hitting the man in front made Michael stumble back, and he wondered if the bullet had traveled straight through his human shield. There was no pain. He just about managed not to fall, but the man in front of him slid down. Before the man could get out a second shot, Miguel had kicked him from his position down on the floor. He swiped the man's legs with his feet, knocking the guy straight down like a bowling pin. Antonio marched towards him and Michael could see straight down the barrel of his gun. Michael had no idea what to do, squeezing the trigger to no effect as Antonio advanced. He thought the anticipation was the worst part until he felt the bullet travel through his shoulder like a red-hot poker.

He stumbled back, hitting the wall before sliding down. He refused to look down as he felt the warmth of blood gush down his front. As he moved, sharp pains radiated across his chest like fork lightning spreading off in a million directions. His brain imagined bone shattered into a million fragments, and everything went fuzzy around the edges.

"I thought about shooting you in the head. But you need to suffer." Antonio smacked him across the top of the head with the butt of his gun and then swung his clenched fist upwards, threatening to separate his jawbone from the rest of his face. Something cracked as his brain reverberated in his skull. Michael wanted to scream so desperately, but his body couldn't make a sound, besides a raspy gargle. His head lolled to the side and he could see Miguel. The rope that had been used to bind him was now wrapped around the other man's neck. The course, twisted fibers digging into the man's neck as his face got deep-red, and then purple.

Samuel aimed his gun towards Miguel, who tried to use the other man to cover himself from bullet-fire. Samuel put a bullet straight through his own hit-man with little emotion and pushed the body to one side. Michael had no idea how he managed it, but Miguel dove to one side and wrenched the gun from Samuel's hand, twisting his arm as he head-butted him with such force, Michael could hear the cracking sound from the other side of the room.

"You killed them, you fucking worm. My wife. My kid. They did nothing to you." He moved the angle of the gun down to his groin area. The deafening reverberations of the bullet were soon drowned out by the howling. The sound of pure, unadulterated pain.

As Tanya made a run for the front door, Antonio left Michael and darted across the room, dragging her back, yanking her arm hard and slapping her into submission. Antonio held Tanya by the hair, keeping her in one place as he went to turn his gun on Miguel at the same time. In the time that Antonio had taken to stop Tanya from escaping,

Miguel had grabbed one of three larges bottles of gasoline that were stashed in the corner. Michael assumed they had planned on burning the evidence afterwards. Miguel tipped the bottle in Antonio's direction, liberally dowsing him in the liquid and accidentally splashing Josie and Tanya in the process.

He came closer until he was pouring it directly over Antonio's head, and once it was empty, he hurled it across the room. Michael hoped that he wouldn't let everyone burn just to get back at Samuel, but he knew he was single-minded and in pain so didn't put it past him.

"You don't want to do that." Antonio spluttered as gasoline dripped from his hair onto his face. The choking reek of chemicals filled the air

"Why the fuck not?" He challenged him.

"Do you not want to know where your daughter is? I know Samuel said she was dead, but—"

Miguel pulled a silver flip lighter from his pocket. "Then you better tell me now or you burn."

"I can take you to her. You and me just need to go for a little drive. Work this thing out. You've been loyal up until now. This can work out for everyone I swear."

Michel wondered if a gunshot could ignite gasoline as he saw Antonio reach for his gun. They looked at each other, trying to figure each other out. Josie ran to Michael, her hands shaking profusely. "Oh god. I'm so sorry." She repeated over and over like a record stuck on a loop. Her sister followed behind her. "Josie, I—"

"Shut up. Just shut up." Josie shouted, taking her cardigan and pressing it against Michael's chest, making him scream with the pressure. "It's okay. It's going to be fine," she muttered as she put a hand on his forehead.

"Is there anything I can do?" Tanya uttered meekly, a look of shame plastered on her face.

"Oh, you've done enough." Josie was trembling now, a combination of fear and rage.

"Why are you even here? I didn't ask you here," said Tanya, as if that would somehow make everything better.

"Because your my sister."

"I loved him. I didn't think. It just happened. It was—"

"Love." Josie laughed spitefully. "You have got to be kidding me. You have no fucking idea what love is… the way you treat people."

"If I'm so terrible, like you always said, then why the hell did you come in the first place?"

"Because that's what people do. They care. They give and give and give. They sacrifice. All I have ever seen you do is take. You kept the money, didn't you? Bankrupted mom and dad, then fucked around with some cartel member of all people."

"It wasn't like that."

"Oh, then do tell me, what exactly was it like. There is no way you can talk your way out of this, justify this. Do you have any idea what you've done?"

As Michael lay there, the sisters' shouting grew faint. He couldn't believe the last words he would hear, would just be hate. Even now, she was too busy arguing to pay attention to what was happening, but then, hadn't he been doing the exact same his entire life. Taking every part of his life, no matter how big or small, and turning it into an argument, a conflict, a battle. Ignoring any good thing, dismissing any compliment. He hadn't been paying attention. Never. But now, he couldn't help but cling onto consciousness, any last bit of awareness he had to keep him anchored to this world. His whole life his sentience had been his greatest curse, but it was all he knew.

Everything happened in slow motion now as he saw Miguel and Antonio struggle, and the flame of the lighter traveled towards the ground. The porous concrete had sucked up the gasoline in like a sponge. The flames came quickly. Starting on the floor, and a whoosh, as the burning energy traveled along the floor, and leaped up Antonio's body, surrounding him in white light. As he dropped to the ground sparks ignited the burlap blanket, taking the body of the first man with it. It didn't take long for smoke to start catching Michael's throat. The room had seemed so bare before, yet there were so many little things dotted around that fueled the fire. Flames spread across the walls, fingers of yellow and orange curling up to the ceiling, leaving a thick blanket of smoke.

The pain in Michael's body when he moved that had forced him to stop trying, had now been surpassed by the pain of the heat of the fire—moving was the lesser of two evils. Josie helped him up, and he did everything he could to avoid passing out. The fire consumed the front of the building so they had no choice but to go out the back.

Miguel saw Josie, Tanya, and Michael stagger in his direction and tried the back door. Locked. He kicked the door at full pelt, cracking the wood, and tearing the frame away from the wall. He kicked again. The flames grew higher as the door burst open. It was becoming impossible to see, and just as they passed to the back of the house, the air grew cooler and cleaner. An old kitchen led to the back door. Almost bare except for some old pots crammed haphazardly onto a wooden shelf. Miguel wrestled with the bars on the exterior door. This door was also locked, and twice as sturdy as the other. He shook the door in desperation, "Come on," he shouted as if trying to reason with the inanimate object.

Josie started pulling wooden drawers out, spilling the contents all over the floor, looking for something to unlock it. "Yes. Miguel. Miguel." She waved a key in the air triumphantly, and he took it from her.

There was a noise. A scream maybe, drowned by the roaring flames. He should probably assume it was Antonio burning alive, but something told him that wasn't the case. Something inside him told him he had to go back. Something called him, and for some reason, he listened. He slipped back into the veil of smoke before anyone could notice and his feet just walked, almost independently of himself, like they knew where he needed to be. Whatever was waiting for him was upstairs.

He burst through the wall of flames as quickly as possible and made his way up the stairs, coughing profusely, wondering if smoke inhalation would finish him off. Now he reached the landing, he could hear Josie cry out his name. "Don't follow me!" He shouted into the crackling roar, hoping she had heard him and didn't do anything stupid. Nothing looked real in the gray filter of smoke that started flooding the stairway. It could have been the lack of oxygen, but he felt high, like nothing could hurt him now. He was invincible. The noise was clearer from upstairs, a banging coming from the end of the hall. A door with a key still in the keyhole. Smoke from downstairs clung around the door like a fog. He wasn't sure how he went from feeling like a warrior, to being on his knees in front of the door. He'd somehow missed a step. His mind was cutting bits out. On fast-forward, he opened the lock from his position of the floor and waited for whatever was on the other-side.

Clutching her knees in a tight ball, was a girl. She looked tiny in the large empty room. Her vulnerability made him feel things he didn't like, a memory maybe, but he wasn't willing to search his mind for an answer. She backed away, scooting across the floor. "It's okay. I'm a friend." He wasn't really sure how to talk to young children. It was like trying to communicate with an alien being that didn't speak his language. She looked so scared of him, and he had no idea how to let her know he was not a threat. Her wide eyes seemed transfixed to one spot —his chest. He looked down, following her eye line and realized how he must have looked. The blood. "It's okay. It's okay," he repeated, holding out a hand. He didn't know if he had the strength to lift her, and whether she would want to be carried. The heat was building. He could feel it rising up from the floor, through the soles of his shoes, as if the rubber could melt any second. "Please."

He tried to reason with her but she stayed put. Without speaking, she grabbed her hand, leading her towards the door and guiding her down the hall. The fire had crept up the stairs, and flames curled around the top of the landing from down below, like waves crashing over a sea-wall. He moved quickly, keeping close to the wall until they made it to the room at the other end.

Once inside he slammed the door shut behind them with his foot. The door handle was far too hot to touch now. He let go of the girl's hand so he could cough. It came from deep within him, almost making him vomit.

He stumbled towards the window and pulled up the shutter, sticking his head out and sucking in the air cool air.

"Michael!" Josie shouted from below him. They stood by the trees, far enough away to be clear of the smoke that streamed from the door below. A look of relief washed over her and she waved her arms at him, even though she had already got his attention. He turned back and scanned the room while the little girl crouched below the window, hugging her knees again. The room was sparse: a few shelves, some abandoned old books, and a bed in the middle.

"I'm going to need your help," he said, looking at the girl, but realizing she didn't speak English. He could have at least learned the world help in Spanish. There wasn't time to stand around berating himself, and he pulled on one corner of the mattress. He tried to pick it up, but the pain crippled him and he got onto his hands and knees, breathing through the pain, waiting for it to subside. Body language was universal. The girl held one end of the mattress and looked at him. Luckily it was a thin mattress or he couldn't imagine she would have the body strength to carry it, and he certainly wouldn't have.

Between them they just about managed to slide the mattress out of the window, and he snatched in a breath after letting the mattress fall and waited for the pain to subside again, but the most painful part wasn't over. He wondered if the mattress was even enough to cushion their fall.

He moved the girl away from the window and looked down, trying to gauge what position to fall in. This was going to hurt like a bitch. Luckily the mattress had fallen close to the house, so he didn't need to jump forward, just fall. He held the girl in front of him and took a backwards leap of faith.

As he felt the air rush past him as he plummeted, he heard screams and then his back made contact with the ground below. For the first few seconds, he could only focus on the pain. Convinced he had fallen short of the mattress, he imagined his spine shattered into a million pieces. It's only when he laid his arms down that he realized he had made it, but every bone in his body still hurt none the less.

The girl jumped out of his arms and as he rested his head to the left, he saw her run into Miguel's arms. They both cried as much as each other and Miguel caught Michael's eyes briefly before stroking his daughter's tangled long hair and then holding her head gently between the palms of his hands, inspecting her face as if checking that she was real. He looked back at Michael and gave him a nod. Such a small gesture, but Michael could see the gratitude radiating from him. It was the kind of nod one soldier might give another before walking towards the front-line. No words would be good enough.

Josie grabbed his uninjured hand, possibly the only part of his body that didn't feel like it was being stabbed by daggers. She hovered over him, blocking out the blinding sun. Behind her he could see smoke, and flames, and embers reaching up to the sky.

Now he could rest. He had done what he needed to do. He couldn't believe that somehow, everything had worked out, although not perfectly. Perfection didn't exist, but it was the best he could have hoped for. He had done something. Not just stood, watching from the shadows. Somehow, now, lying on the floor in agony was the most content he had ever been. Josie babbled about how everything would be okay.

Didn't she realize everything was already okay? His hand touched her wrist, and he looked in her eyes. "You have to forgive her. If you don't this will all be for nothing." The sound of sirens pierced through the frayed edges of his awareness. Everything muted slightly, including the pain, which he was grateful for. He wondered if he was hallucinating as Aleksander came running from the side of the house with two people following him—a man and a woman in uniform with medical supplies.

"I'm sorry I left. I had to come back." He knelt down beside Josie and their faces blurred into one.

Chapter Thirty Eight

Everything had been awkward. They barely spoke a word the entire time: not on the way to the airport, not on the flight, not as they disembarked, not when they went through customs. She couldn't bring herself to speak, as she feared what she might say. They waited at the luggage carousel and Josie watched the bags roll past her. Usually, she was strangely lucky, and her bag would always pop from behind the plastic flaps quickly, but Tanya's bag refused to show. Josie had no belongings to check in, as Samuel had burned them all, yet Tanya had a massive suitcase to collect. It made her furious that she had nothing left, yet Tanya did. She resented having to wait for Tanya's baggage and just wanted to go home and lie in bed, staring at the wall.

Tanya excused herself to go to the toilet, and now Josie was alone, the tears came out of nowhere. She tried to wipe them away quickly to avoid bringing attention to herself. The last thing she wanted was for someone to ask her what was wrong, as that would set her off even more. Through her wet, blurry eyes she saw her sister's bag come around. It's bright colorful pattern taunting her. The weight of it made her whole body heave as she dragged it off of the carousel and lugged it towards the seat. Left holding the bag. Typical. She would have laughed if she wasn't so angry.

Tanya emerged from the bathroom and kept her eyes to the ground as she shuffled along. Josie wished she would hurry up, and sighed. There was nothing her sister could do that wouldn't piss her off.

"Let's go." Josie demanded and took the lead as she headed for the exit. She was safe now. Her family was somehow complete again, yet more broken than ever. The safety should have been a relief, yet she felt hollow. It was busy in the arrivals lounge, as people dashed around and others held up boards with people's names on. It had all the frenetic energy of the trading floor on Wall Street.

There they were. Her parent's faces emerged through the crowd. The wide grins on their faces made her want to cry again. They had no idea. In their minds, their beloved daughter miraculously escaped the jaws of death and was to magically reappear in their lives. Innocent, ignorant, completely unaware that their own daughter had staged her own kidnapping to rinse them for all they were worth. It just occurred to Tanya that they had requested such a specific amount, an amount so high that, unless you knew the family you might not expect them to have that sort of money to hand, yet not so high to make it impossible for them to pay. The calculated, manipulative nature of what she had done made Josie want to tell everyone. They deserved to know.

"Babies. My babies." Her mom cried straight away and came towards them with open arms, embracing them both at the same time, one daughter in each arm. Josie looked over her mom's shoulder to see her dad's face, stoic as usual. Tanya then went to hug her father. She had always been a daddy's girl, well, when she wanted something. Josie tried to keep the disgust from her face. She could probably explain away all her weird looks. She's in shock, traumatized. She couldn't be expected to behave normally; to feel the things that she should be feeling right then.

Michael's words bounced in her ears. She would forgive her, eventually, but now was not that time. She promised she wouldn't tell their parent's what she had done, but she owed her. She owed her parent's. She owed everyone. Josie would ensure Tanya spent the rest of her life repenting. Her parents were so happy; it wasn't worth telling them the ugly truth. She imagined the look on their faces if they were ever to find out. Her dad would explode. Everything would be even worse.

"My brave girl. My brave, brave girl." Her mom clutched Tanya close to her at every opportunity she got on the way to the car, and Josie resisted the urge to scoff. "I'm never letting you out of my sight again."

Being trapped at home with the family, not off traveling the world, would probably be Tanya's idea of prison, and as close as she would get to being incarcerated. Why couldn't she just be grateful for what she had? Why did she have to do what she did? Josie couldn't fathom why, but couldn't bring herself to ask Tanya for an explanation. No reason she could offer would be good enough.

When they got to the car, their father shoved Tanya's luggage in the trunk, and even opened the back door for her. "She's not an invalid dad." Josie snapped.

"Have some respect, Josie. She's been through a lot. Not everyone is as strong as you." Her mom weighed in.

Josie bit down on her lip and dug her nails into the palms of her hands. It took every last bit of restraint not to explode.

"Get in the car. What's wrong with you?" her mom asked.

"Nothing." A single word was all she could muster, and she got in the back seat, slamming the car door behind her and yanking at the seat belt.

"Careful." Her father raised his voice. "This car is new."

"I know what's wrong." He mother announced from the front passenger seat. "Sorry we doubted you, Josie. We still think it was stupid what you did, but you saved your sister's life and me and your dad will never forget that. Why don't we take you to that frozen yogurt place you love so much, or that Italian restaurant? You know, the one by the park. You deserve it."

Frozen yogurt. The words sounded ridiculous. Frozen yogurt wasn't going to make everything better. She resisted the urge to take her anger out on her parent's and responded with another one-word answer. "Maybe." She looked out the window as they drove out of the airport parking lot and let her mind wander. Being in the present was too painful, and she had no idea how she would get past this.

"We still can't believe what you've been through, Tanya. We never gave up hope." Their mom reached her arm from the front seat and squeezed Tanya's shoulder.

"Thanks mom." Tanya held her mom's hand against her shoulder and smiled at her lovingly. What an actress, Josie thought, looking on at the display. It was going to be so hard to survive this if she didn't follow Michael's advice. It had only been a few days and already the anger seemed to have changed her into a different person, a person she didn't like. It was such an ugly emotion and it wouldn't change anything.

It was too late now. She tried to recall that saying. Anger is like swallowing poison and expecting the other person to die. She repeated the words over and over, trying to believe them, yet it still simmered under the surface, waiting for the worst time to burst out of her.

Chapter Thirty Nine

She had to be close now. It was only supposed to be a couple of miles away from the school. She checked her Satellite Navigation again. The place was so big there was more than one entry point. Finally, finding a place to park up, she leaned over to the passenger seat and nudged Aleksander awake.

"We're here." He looked so peaceful, and she felt bad waking him up. She'd picked him up from the airport and they headed straight for the cemetery. The ruffled hair and puffy eyes were the epitome of jet-lag, but there was no time to spare. As she got out of the car and shut the door, Alex stretched his legs. Being cramped on a plane, and then in her little car had taken its toll.

The sunlight caressed her face with its warmth and she looked out across the large expanse of grass and across to the still lake. Rows and rows of gray tombstones stretched into the distance. Some crosses, some rounded. Thick bands in the grass from the mower trails led to a mausoleum standing tall at the far end of the cemetery. The palm trees cast shadows across the perfectly cut grass. It felt peaceful here. It felt right.

She tried to make peace with Tanya, but she wouldn't let her come here. Josie had done her best to respect Michael's wishes. They told the police that Tanya had been held against her will by Antonio and they didn't question this. It was the only way to keep the family together. There was no reason to let her parents feel the pain that came with realizing that someone you cared for could screw you over so utterly. The remorse was obvious. It seeped from Tanya's pores like alcohol, the day after the night before. It was always there, an unspoken truth between them. The self-serving bravado was gone, and Tanya had spent the last year trying to make things right. A changed woman. So there Josie was. Covering for Tanya again. Letting her get away with murder.

"This is the one." Alex stopped. Josie had been so caught up in her own head she barely knew where she was. She stood before Michael's grave. His death was on Antonio's head. It was on Samuel's, Tanya's, and it was on Josie's too. The sad thing was, he probably would have thanked her. He got what he wanted. She often wondered what it would have been like if he had made it that day. Would he have still felt the same way? Could they have found a way to be happy? Deep down, she already knew the answer to that question. The lesson she chose to take was that there was no point delaying the things that she wanted to do. Life was short. She had spent her whole life trying to be the antithesis of her sister, but that was the wrong way to look at it. Her sister had spent her whole life doing what she wanted, and now it was Josie's turn. If only she knew what it was she wanted to do.

"Ready?" Alex pulled a bottle of tequila from his man-bag and sat down on the floor, pouring one shot glass for himself, and one for Michael. He placed the shot glass on the stone.

Josie sat on the soft grass and poured herself a shot, tequila spilling over the side of the glass, leaving sticky residue on her fingers. The dappled sunlight filtered through a towering ever-green overhead, leaving dabs of light and dark across the words carved in the headstone Josie had chosen. A buzz vibrated in her pocket, and Josie slipped out her phone. Tanya's name flashed up on her screen. "Not today." Josie muttered under her breath and went to put her phone back, when it buzzed again with another message from her sister. She decided to read it so she could then forget about it.

Josie.

I have something to tell you. I waited until you went away as I knew you'd be mad, and I wanted you to have some time to cool off before we talked. That article in

the newspaper. Someone has approached me and asked me to write about my experiences. A novel. They offered me an advance. Money's been tight. I had to accept. I hope you understand.

"You've got to be kidding me." Josie's voice cut through the peace and quiet of the cemetery, sending a bird flying up from a tree above.

"What's wrong?" Alex sat up straight.

"Never mind." She kept it to herself. She was not going to let Tanya ruin today. It was too important. "You know what we should do?" she said.

Alex looked at her, waiting for her suggestion.

"We should finish this whole bottle. Screw it. We can drive back tomorrow. There's a place to stay not far from here."

"Cheers to that." He poured them another glass each and raised it up.

She knew it was just a hunk of stone and some ashes buried below, but she wanted to spend as much time there as she could. The burn of the tequila took her back a year. Back to Mexico. Back to the Tulum. She tried to claw back the fading memories. There was a moment that she had considered not asking to sit down next to the lonely-looking guy at the hotel bar, and to take her drinks to her room. In some ways, she was glad she asked to take that chair, to know this person, if only for a short time. She wondered if he would have let her sit with him if he knew how it was going to end up, but yet again, she already knew the answer to that question.